BILLIONAIRE IN VEGAS

BILLIONAIRE MATCHMAKER
BOOK ONE

SUMMER COOPER

LOVY BOOKS

PROLOGUE

"I hate you!"

"That's right. Let it all out. Tell me how you really feel, princess."

I hated it when he called me princess. Gritting my teeth, I selected the book nearest me and tossed it at him with all the force I could muster. He caught it easily and laughed at me which only served to piss me off even more.

"Good throw, princess. Too bad you didn't hit your targ—"

He didn't get the last word out as the box of Kleenex smacked him on the forehead knocking him back in such a comical fashion, I couldn't help but laugh.

"How's that for a target, princess?" I said, taunting him as he held a hand to his forehead looking bewildered.

"Did you seriously just assault me with a box of tissue?"

Instantly, I felt contrite, but I wasn't backing down. I tilted my chin up defiantly. "Yep. That just happened."

"You're going to pay for that," he said, coming towards me, the towel around his hips parting ever so deliciously every time he took a step. He was naked beneath the towel, of course, and I'd be lying if I said it wasn't incredibly difficult to resist taking a peek.

It was then I admitted to myself something my body had known all along. I wanted Jude Foster. And as he backed me into a wall and placed an arm on either side of my head, it wasn't anger I saw there in his eyes, it was lust. I wanted Jude, but he wanted me more.

I could feel the heat emanating from his body. The sexy scent of his aftershave was wreaking havoc on my libido. And his body...Oh God, his body. He was so gorgeous, so perfect. Nothing but solid muscle covered by skin so deliciously smooth I wanted to lick it. I wanted to lick him. All over. He brought his hips to rest against mine and I sucked in a breath.

His sex nestled against my own and I involuntarily shifted against it. He groaned and looked down.

"Do that again," he said, "and I might not be able to control myself..."

I was done being afraid, so without another thought, I rubbed my pelvis against his. Slowly. Languidly.

Taking my time to get intimately acquainted with his sex that apparently loved the attention.

With a growl, he turned me around and in the same motion shoved my robe up around my hips. I felt his cock press against my bare butt as he said against my ear, "Bend over Lacey, it's time for us to become better acquainted."

Without thinking I opened my mouth wide and stuck the length of the divine thickness into my mouth and then slowly pulled back, licking the tip as I looked up.

"What?" I said to my two friends who sat across from me looking amused.

"With technique like that, why in the world did Evan ever leave you?" Emmaline, my friend since kindergarten, said wryly as she stared at me with amusement filled eyes.

I rolled my eyes, "Stop being gross. This popsicle is delicious. You know I haven't had carbs in—"

"Six months... we know, we know," Misha cut in. She was married to an electrical engineer who owned his own engineering firm. She was the wealthiest person I knew, but her clothes belied that fact. I could see a hole near the neck of her blouse and her jeans were faded in a non-fashionable way. I bet the hole was from the stapler where the thrift store workers had stapled the price into the garment and, of course, Misha had haphazardly ripped it out leaving a hole behind. But I knew she didn't care. As long as she didn't pay full price, she was happy. She wasn't only the wealthiest person I knew, she was also the cheapest.

"From the way she was eating that popsicle, if I had to guess I'd say she also hasn't been with a man in about twice as long. Poor girl is going through a sex drought," Misha said, unable to resist teasing me.

"Misha, please...we're in public..." I hissed.

"Don't shush me, you were the one deep throating a popsicle like a porn star."

I blushed.

"Frankly, Lacey, I'm embarrassed for the popsicle. You didn't even take it out for a nice dinner or anything."

I tossed my napkin at her. She dodged it easily, but it fell into the plate of the guest immediately behind her.

My eyes widened in panic. I immediately began to mumble, "I am so sorry, sir. I'll pay for that."

The sir in question took his time withdrawing my balled up napkin from his now unappetizing dessert. I winced as he dropped it with a plop next to his plate and then he looked at me. His eyes were the same color as the chocolate popsicle I'd been devouring. And if I were being honest with myself, he looked just as delicious.

With his large hands, olive complexion, bedroom eyes and thick lashes, I found myself enthralled and instantly feeling inadequate. He was a beautiful specimen of masculinity. Nope. Definitely not my type. Then why was my pulse skipping a beat?

"Maybe if you hadn't been so busy performing sexual favors on that ice cream concoction, you'd have seen me sitting here."

My mouth dropped open and I struggled to come up with something to say when I heard Misha laugh. I shot her a glare.

"I don't know what you're talking about," I said stiffly, raising my chin and looking down my nose at him. It was my signature move whenever I was feeling insecure. I would pretend to be high and mighty when really I wanted to hide my face in a dinner napkin and run away.

The man stood up and instantly my friends' giggles stopped as they watched him approach. He was tall, at least 6'4 and he moved effortlessly in his close-fitting black shirt and expertly tailored dark jeans. My shoulders tensed and I forced myself to appear aloof and unaffected by his size, but more so unaffected by his presence. After all, he was just a man like any other... except sexier. I didn't get a chance to admonish myself for having those thoughts, when he then bent down and said against my ear, "If you ever need any help getting out of that drought, I wouldn't mind being of assistance."

He turned to Misha and Emmaline, saying, "Enjoy dessert, ladies—I know I did."

And with that, he walked out of the restaurant.

Misha barely waited for him to disappear before saying, "Oh my God, he was gorgeous. If I'd known throwing trash around a fancy ice-cream shop would get the attention of a beautiful man like that, I'd throw all the trash."

"Uh huh," Emmaline nodded in agreement. "What did he say to you just now?"

"I hope it was something dirty," Misha said.

"He apologized for getting upset," I said, trying to keep a straight face, but it was no use. My friends knew me too well.

"You're a terrible liar, Lacey," Emmaline said with a laugh.

I shrugged and promptly changed the subject, but in the back of my mind was the feel of the man's breath against my ear.

LATER THAT WEEK, I made my way to the temp office to meet with my recruiter. I did mostly contract work, going from one client to another. I enjoyed it. I didn't like routine or staying in one place, so temp work was great for someone like me. My recruiter, Kadija, had called me last weekend, telling me to report in because she had an opportunity that I'd love. I was a little apprehensive. Kadija had a habit of assigning me the most difficult of clients. I normally didn't complain because it meant the pay was even more, but I wanted to take it easy. I wasn't feeling as motivated to deal with difficult people lately. I figured it was because I was getting older and crankier... even though I was just turning 30 not 70.

I tugged at my earrings nervously as I got into the elevator. I was terribly claustrophobic, but my therapist had suggested I face my fears straight on in order to get better. Emmaline was my therapist and she was currently in graduate school online earning her master's degree in psychology. I didn't know if her advice was any good or not, but it was free.

I sighed in relief when the elevator dinged, signaling we'd arrived at my floor and I practically jumped out of it, heading in the direction of the temp agency. I found the frosted glass door, pushed it open, and before I could even approach the window to sign in, the receptionist smiled widely at me and said, "Don't sit. Go straight in."

I raised my eyebrows and did as I was told.

Normally, I read all the outdated magazines in the lobby before Kadija made an appearance.

Speak of the devil, she met me immediately as I entered.

"Lacey Cabot. Now if you aren't a sight for sore eyes." She gave me a big hug as if we hadn't seen each other in years, when actually it couldn't have been more than three months.

I hugged her back, no matter how uncomfortable it made me. I hated hugs from strangers and yes, I'd known Kadija for a couple of years now, but I didn't even hug my aunt who'd practically raised me. Actually, my aunt didn't hug anyone. She was a stoic woman. I tried my best to take after her, but I wore my emotions on my sleeves, no matter how hard I tried to hide them.

As expected, Kadija could see that I was surprised. She smiled at me, showing off her deep dimples in her flawless caramel-colored face. Her hair was in dreadlocks and artfully arranged in a bun on top of her head. She smiled at me as if she had the best secret she could barely contain.

"I know, I know. I practically tackled you when you walked in, but Lacey, I got a call from a friend of a friend who is looking for a personal assistant. It's a great opportunity for you!"

I frowned. "A personal assistant gig? That's not my

thing." I had an issue with the idea of being at someone's beck and call.

"You don't have any office work or something along those lines?"

"He'll pay you seventy-five dollars an hour."

I blinked. "Excuse me?"

Kadija smiled like the Cheshire Cat. "Uh huh. Now you change your tune. Come on, step into my office."

I followed her silently in a state of shock. What person in their right mind would pay some stranger seventy-five dollars an hour to just do menial tasks like fetching the dry-cleaning and paying their utility bill? I narrowed my eyes.

"Who's the client? Isn't that a lot, even for a personal assistant? It must be someone crazy difficult."

"Not at all. I promise you that." Kadija smiled in an assuring manner from the opposite side of the desk.

I didn't believe her and I said as much. "Come on, Kadija. Seventy-five bucks an hour? For how long?"

"Oh...well...indefinitely," she said, pulling at the sleeve of her blouse.

I didn't like the sound of that. "So let me get this right, someone indefinitely needs a personal assistant and is willing to pay me seventy-five dollars an hour for my services?"

She nodded, "I know it sounds crazy—"

"Yep."

She continued, "But it's a legitimate job."

"Tell me about the client."

She smiled in relief, probably thinking my curiosity would get the best of me. "His name is Oliver Foster. His personal assistant just recently retired so they're looking for a replacement. Have you heard of the Foster family?"

I shook my head. "Should I have?"

Kadija shrugged, "They're one of the oldest families in the area. They keep a pretty low-profile."

I made a noncommittal sound and Kadija continued, "My source tells me he's a harmless old man who just needs a little companionship."

"Sounds a little like an escort service—"

Kadija tossed her hands up. "At least try to work with me here, Lacey. I'm offering you the opportunity of a lifetime and didn't your car just die?"

She was referring to my early 90s Honda. I loved that car and I had been too cheap to replace it. I didn't like the idea of taking out an auto loan, so when my car had died, I started taking the bus everywhere instead. I wasn't enjoying it. Public transportation drove me crazy. I didn't like all the people sitting so close to me, randomly talking to me or having to reach over people to signal for my stop. I hated it, but I hated the idea of debt more. I watched my aunt struggle with debt while she raised me and I didn't want to repeat that experience in my own life. For the most part, I was a practical person and I didn't like complications.

"Yes, my car died," I admitted with a sigh.

"And for the amount of money you'll make working as Mr. Foster's assistant you'll be able to buy a car with cash or at least put down a nice down payment pretty soon…"

She had a point but I wasn't going to tell her, and then she sweetened the deal. "I heard he gives bonuses."

I kept my expression as impassive as I could before saying, "Oh really? Cash bonuses?"

"His previous personal assistant made an extra five thousand a month on top of their salary."

"Five thousand dollars?"

Kadija nodded, now looking smug. "So are you in? If so, I can arrange a meeting later today."

"That would be great," I said, relenting. Beggars can't be choosy, as my aunt would say, and hey, I needed the money.

Kadija clapped her hands together like a gleeful toddler and thanked me. She then slid a card over to me. I took it curiously and realized that it was a hand-written card with an address and a code on it.

"What's this?"

"Mr. Foster's address and security code. He's expecting you."

I still felt a little hesitant, but then I thought back to

my bus ride to the temp office. There'd been a guy on there who kept insisting on singing to me. And when I'd blatantly ignored him, he had tried to spit shine my shoe. Or at least, I was giving him the benefit of the doubt that he was trying to shine my shoes and not necessarily trying to spit on me. Yeah, I needed a new car. I needed Mr. Foster's money.

Kadija was nice enough to call me a taxi and less than thirty minutes later, we pulled up in front of Mr. Foster's estate. There was a security guard out front who beckoned for us to pull up.

He lowered himself to our line of vision and said through the window, "Are you Miss Cabbage?"

"Cabot," I corrected tightly, blushing ever so slightly. I didn't think my last name was that difficult to pronounce.

He gave a self-deprecating laugh and shook his head. He scratched at his long beard and said with a little smile, "Sorry about that Miss Cabot. I'm terrible with names. I have two daughters and I mix them up all the time! And their names sound nothing alike."

I smiled slightly at his attempt to be friendly and told myself to stop being so uptight. "It's okay. It happens."

He then surprised me saying, "Miss Cabot, ummm cars aren't allowed on the property. You'll need to walk to the entrance."

"Walk?" I said looking down dubiously at my feet. I wasn't exactly wearing walking shoes.

The security guard looked apologetic as he opened the door for me and I slid out. I paid the driver who watched the entire exchange wordlessly before driving off.

"How far away is the actual estate?" I said unable to tell since the large gate was covered in ivy and I couldn't see through the bars to the house on the opposite side.

"About half a mile," the guard said, and my mouth fell open.

"You have got to be kidding me," I mumbled. I wasn't the athletic type. My idea of working out was lifting a spoon full of ice cream to my face to shove into my mouth. I was lucky I had skinny genes, because I was a lazy glutton to be completely honest.

"Maybe it's only a quarter mile—"

"That doesn't sound much better."

"Okay. Well, it's definitely less than ten minutes."

"I can't believe this."

"Could be worse," the guard said with a smile. He then walked to his little office and hit a button, the gate opened and suddenly I felt nervous. What was I getting myself into?

"Just follow the path straight up... you can't miss it."

"Sure. Great. Thanks, ummm—" I realized then that I hadn't asked his name.

"It's Peter. Peter Nguyen. You can call me Pete. Everyone does."

"Nice to meet you, Pete. And please, call me Lacey."

He smiled and shook my hand. "You better head on up. He's going to wonder what's taking so long."

"Oh yeah, you're right. Well, wish me luck. Hopefully, I won't be too much of a sweaty mess when I get there."

He shrugged. "Trust me, Mr. Foster either won't notice or won't care."

"He's a pretty laissez-faire type of boss?" I asked hopefully.

"Mr. Foster's a character."

I wanted to ask more, but I needed to get a move on so I waved my goodbye to Pete and started up the path to the estate. And it was then that I saw that the ground wasn't flat at all. It was hilly.

"You have got to be kidding me," I said out loud as I made my way up the first hill, huffing and puffing as I went. I knew I should have been impressed by the beauty around me; the immaculately kept lawn, the overhanging trees along the path that must have been hundreds of years old, the gardens that begged to be on the cover of a gardening magazine.

But I was miserable. The flowers aggravated my allergies and made my nose run. My eyes were watering and I couldn't stop sneezing. My calves were on fire and

I felt sweat running down my thighs. My granny panties were uncomfortably tugging in weird places and I hazarded a look behind me just to be sure no one was watching as I reached under my skirt and attempted to tug them back into place. And it was then that I heard the laugh.

Startled, I looked to where it had come from and saw a man standing there with a smug smile on his face.

I could feel myself blushing as I opened my mouth to explain myself, but then I promptly closed it as the man grew nearer. I immediately took a step back. I recognized him and if the stupid smile on his face was any indication, he clearly recognized me.

"Please tell me you're not Mr. Foster."

He smiled widely at me. "Hate to disappoint you, but I am."

2

———

I didn't say a word—I just turned around and marched away, determined to put this whole day behind me.

"Woah, whoa, whoa, where are you going?" said the man who I recognized as the sexy stranger from the ice cream shop. He attempted to keep up with me, so I willed myself to walk faster. It didn't work. I was already spent from walking up the first two hills and my muscles were screaming in protest.

"Home." I struggled to get just that one word since I was almost panting in exhaustion.

"So you're just going to leave?"

"Yep," I said, trying to maintain my dignity as I stumbled over a rock and barely stayed upright.

"Is walking new for you?"

I shot him a glare. "Is being a decent human being new for you?"

"Ouch," he said, attempting to look injured, but failing miserably.

I ignored him and continued marching away. He tried to keep up with me and I walked faster. I knew I was huffing and puffing, and I felt even more humiliated because I was apparently really out of shape.

"Hmmm.... maybe you should slow down," he said easily, not at all winded.

"You—can't tell—me—what—to—do," I said between breaths. Apparently, I couldn't walk quickly and talk at the same time. My heart was beating fast and I could feel sweat collecting across my forehead. With frustration, I wiped at it.

"You need a handkerchief?"

"No—I—need—you—to—just—leave—me—alone!" I managed to yell, again having to pause between words, which served to make my plea to be left alone even weaker.

"You look like you're going to pass out. Do you have some sort of health condition?"

"Hey! What's that supposed to mean?" I said, stopping and turning in his direction. I planted my hands on my hips and tilted my head to glare up at him. Being just five feet tall wasn't helping me feel in control of the situation, especially since I struggled to control my own breathing. Honestly, I hadn't stopped to confront him because I was offended by his words, I just thought I was going to pass out if I didn't stop walking.

"Jude, I gave you one task and you managed to completely make a mess of things," came a voice from in front of us.

I TURNED in the direction of the voice and couldn't help but smile. In front of me was an older man with a big bushy white mustache and a bald head. He was wearing brief shorts and pumping his legs back and forth. I guess he had just got back from exercising. He was shirtless and his chest sort of caved inwards. He looked like a baby bird. And when he smiled, I saw that he had a large gap in between his two front teeth.

"Dad, I said I would take care of it and I was," the guy from the ice cream shop said with annoyance.

"Well, apparently you aren't taking care of it, because she's obviously walking in the opposite direction of the house."

"I'm sorry, I'm not sure what's going on here, but I'm leaving," I said turning away from them both and continuing my way to the entrance. Pete saw me and gave a hesitant wave in greeting, before seeing who accompanied me.

"Uh oh," I saw him mouth.

The shirtless older man stepped in front of me, blocking me from leaving. He gave me an apologetic smile, saying, "You must be Ms. Cabot. I'm sorry for my son's behavior. He doesn't know how to talk to women, that's why he's currently single."

Ice cream shop guy responded, "Excuse my father. He, unfortunately, has no excuse for himself. I wish I could call him senile, but that would be giving him too much credit."

There was no humor in his voice and the tension between the two of them instantly made me wish I had never stepped out of the taxi.

"Well, umm... I hope you guys figure everything out..." I said, gesturing for Pete to open the gate.

The older Mr. Foster immediately looked contrite, "I'm sorry, Ms. Cabot. I'm Oliver. Oliver Foster. And you've already met my son, Jude. I hope not by reputation—"

"Nice, Dad. Contrary to popular belief I've only slept with a quarter of the women in this state, not all of them," Jude said sarcastically, folding his arms across his body.

I got the feeling their argument was less about me and more about something I had no involvement in.

I looked from father to son and said to Oliver, "So you're my prospective client? Not Jude?"

Oliver nodded, "Jude was supposed to meet up with

you and escort you to the house. Apparently, that task was much too hard."

"If you cared so much about what I could do right, you could have met up with Ms. Cabot on your own."

"Apparently..."

Now I was feeling like a third wheel and I saw that Pete had the gate open. "Well, gentlemen, it's been a blast. I hope you guys settle whatever this all is," I said, gesturing between the two of them.

Oliver stopped me, saying, "We're sorry, Ms. Cabot. I'm afraid our manners are lacking. Please stay."

I looked at Jude who seemed to want to be anywhere else but in the presence of his father. Then what was he doing here?

"Not to be too personal, but do both of you live here? Would I be working as a personal assistant for the both of you?"

"Are you kidding me? I'm not the old, senile one," Jude said with a dry laugh.

Oliver's expression became tight. "Trust me, my dear, I wouldn't subject you to that type of torture. You were hired as my assistant. Jude can fend for himself."

Jude gave a harsh laugh. "You got that right."

I glanced again at Oliver. Despite his obvious contempt towards his son, I didn't think he seemed too bad. I figured if I were related to Jude, I would hate him too. My mind made up, I said, "Well if that's the case, I guess we can give this a shot."

Oliver grinned and folded his hands in as if praying and bowed to me. "You won't regret it, Ms. Cabot."

"Please, just call me Lacey."

He took my hand, raised it to his lips and kissed it. "A pleasure to meet you, Lacey."

HALF AN HOUR LATER, I found myself seated across from Jude. I tried to avoid looking directly at him even though it was nearly impossible. The stupid look on his face made me want to roll my eyes in annoyance. The look was a cross between a smirk and gloating. And more bothersome was that I still found him just as sexy now as when I first encountered him in the ice cream shop. I was so annoyed with myself.

"I hope you're not a vegetarian, Ms. Cabot," Oliver said, as a butler appeared from nowhere and began to serve lunch. We were sitting in the expansive dining room and I was still trying to get over how much I was surrounded by wealth. The house was easily 10,000 square feet and the most endearing room in my mind was the library. He had taken me on a tour of the main house while lunch was prepared and it had been over-whelming.

"I definitely enjoy meat. I'm a huge carnivore."

"I can believe that."

I ignored Jude's comment, refusing to acknowledge the innuendo paired with his not so innocent look.

I cleared my throat and pointedly turned my attention to the senior Foster. "If you don't mind me asking, what type of business are you in, sir?"

"Please call me, Oliver," he said, wiping his mouth with a napkin. "And my business entails a lot of things."

"Our family earned its money the old-fashioned way. Inherited."

Mr. Oliver chuckled at Jude's interjection. "He's right. My great-grandfather made a few excellent investments and since then not a member of this family has actually had to work for a living since."

"Wow."

"Don't be too impressed. Jude here knows how to spend money faster than the Treasury can print it."

"I do my best."

"Don't we know it."

The tension between the two of them made me uncomfortable, but I wasn't going to say anything. I needed this job and Jude wouldn't always be around, at least, I hoped he wouldn't.

"But enough about us, let's talk about you, Lacey. I love your name by the way. It's very lady-like. It truly fits you. Women nowadays can be so gauche, but you, you're so classy."

Jude shot me a grin that clearly told me he was thinking of our encounter in the restaurant the other day or earlier when I was picking my underwear out of my butt. I narrowed my eyes at him and thanked his father for the compliment, although I felt it was border-line sexist.

"I have my moments," I said with a shrug.

"So where are you from, Lacey? And why aren't you gainfully employed?" Jude asked as he cut into his steak and took a huge bite. I secretly hoped he would choke on it. But of course, he didn't.

I'm sure I was glowering as I went to answer his rude question, but Oliver cut in, "Excuse my son. He was just leaving anyway, weren't you, Jude?"

"Nope. I think I can spare a minute or two."

They silently stared at each other, waiting for the other to back down when Oliver sighed and said, "Must you drive me insane all the time?"

"It's what I live for, father dear." Jude's tone dripped with veiled hostility and sarcasm. I rethought my earlier feelings. They didn't just dislike each other. They hated each other.

I felt uncomfortable so I began to speak, hoping that would detract from the tension. "What would you like to know about me, Oliver? I'm a pretty open book. I'm assuming Kadija sent you my resume."

"Oh yes, but a resume can only tell you so much about a person."

I nodded, "Well, to answer your earlier question, Jude, I'm from a small town outside of Georgia."

"Really? You don't have a discernible Southern accent."

I shrugged, not daring to mention that my accent had been the bane of my college existence when I went to school up north, surrounded by people who hadn't ever heard a Southerner talk in "real life". I had grown tired of being an oddity and had worked hard to eliminate the Southern twang.

I didn't say this to the Fosters though. I moved on to the next question. "And I think I'm pretty gainfully employed, after all, I'm working for your father."

Oliver smiled. "And I'm so happy to have you."

"Cheers to that," Jude said unexpectedly. I raised my wine glass with the other two and ignored Jude as he winked at me.

Abruptly he downed the rest of his wine in one gulp, wiped his mouth across his sleeve and stood up. "Well, Father, Miss Cabot, it's been fun but I have to go."

"Work's calling?" I said deliberately being intrusive. Tit-for-tat as far as I was concerned.

"Nope. Women to chase," Oliver quipped. "You know Jude here was a professional soccer player. Although I think he spent most of his time chasing women instead of focusing on the game."

Jude said, "A bit of both. I like mixing business with pleasure."

"Yeah. Don't we know it."

As if he didn't even hear his father, Jude walked away without another word. I watched him leave. I couldn't help myself as I checked out his butt. It definitely belonged to an athlete. And as if he felt my eyes on him, he turned around and shot me a meaningful grin before disappearing through the dining room doors.

Oliver shook his head and gestured to the butler for more wine. After he was done filling up the glass, he went to leave, but Oliver stopped him saying, "Just leave the bottle. I'll need it."

The butler walked away with a little smile.

"I have to apologize for my son. He's a little bit of an asshole. Well, actually more than a little bit."

I choked into my wine and Oliver looked at me with amusement.

After I was done coughing, I struggled to come up with something nice to say. I tried to be considerate. "I'm sure he has his moments."

"Not many of them," Oliver said without any animosity. There was mostly amusement in his voice. His expression became serious. "We don't see eye to eye on most things, but he's still my son. I did a crappy job raising him, so apparently his being an asshole is mostly my fault."

"I'm sure you did the best you could," I said, not knowing what else to say.

"That's not what my therapist says," Oliver said with a laugh.

I liked Oliver. I liked his frank way of speaking and his self-deprecating humor.

"Anyway, I'm sure you didn't become a personal assistant to listen to a rich old person's problem."

"Actually, I'm sure that's exactly what you're paying me for."

He laughed and said, "You're right."

I reached for my purse and pulled out my tablet. I turned it on and said, "So should we start off with a list of tasks you would like me to complete and perhaps we can share calendars and sync your contact lists?"

"All that sounds great. I love technology. My previous personal assistant wrote everything down on a notepad."

I laughed as if I didn't do that too. I only reached for my tablet before I left the house because I couldn't find my notepad.

Oliver and I covered the basics of the job for about an hour. I asked a lot of questions that he really couldn't answer, but I got to know more about him. He was a really dear old man. I didn't know what he'd been like as a father, but as an employer, it was clear that he was going to be one of my favorite clients. *Thanks, Kadija.*

Afterward, he gave me a tour of other areas around his home, the stables, guest house, swimming pool and gardens, and a series of passwords he wanted me to commit to memory; he insisted I didn't write them down.

Later that afternoon, I packed my purse ready to leave.

"So what time tomorrow would you like me to stop by?"

"Don't you have a birthday coming up this weekend?"

I looked at him, surprised. "How did you know?"

He replied, "Your personnel file."

"Oh yeah. I have some plans but nothing really concrete." I was lying. I didn't have anything planned. Even though Emmaline and Misha had offered to take me out for the weekend, we hadn't actually come up with exciting stuff to do. We'd probably just sit around my house and drink some beer.

"That's too bad. A young girl like yourself should celebrate. Do something special. After all, you only turn twenty-one once." He winked at me then and it reminded me so much of Jude's wink earlier. Maybe he had gotten his rakishness from his father after all, I thought, amused.

"I'm turning thirty, as we both know, and honestly, it's no big deal."

"Maybe not to you..." Oliver said turning away from me and walking towards the study. I followed behind him, wondering where he was going so abruptly.

He found his phone and tapped a few buttons and the next thing I knew, my phone beeped. I reached for it and my eyes grew wide at the message there. It was an alert from an app that we had agreed upon for payment purposes and according to the notification, Oliver had wired me $5000.

I opened my mouth and sputtered, "Is this some sort of payment advance?"

"No. It's a bonus."

"But I haven't even done any work yet."

He shrugged it off. "I'm sure you'll do great. Consider it an investment. A happy, rested assistant is a good assistant. So take the weekend off, on me. Do something fun. Go to Vegas! Or Monte Carlo!"

I laughed. "Hold your horses. You gave me five thousand, not ten thousand."

Oliver laughed, "I have a hotel in Vegas, if you want to go there you'll have free accommodations and of course, you have access to my private plane."

I shook my head. "I couldn't—"

"I insist."

I was about to say no and then thought to myself –

why not? I didn't have any solid plans. And that had been my own fault since I'd insisted on not having a party even though both Emmaline and Misha were more than willing to plan one.

I frowned as I thought about the choices I tended to make. For some reason, I always deprived myself of any fun. When had I become such a stick in the mud? Oh yeah, I'd always been one. But no more. I was turning over a new leaf, with my employer's blessing and money, obviously. I would be stupid to say no and so I said yes.

I thanked Oliver profusely and waited while he called me a taxi. As I walked to meet the taxi, I pulled out my cellphone and texted Emmaline and Misha. "We're going to Vegas, ladies!!!!"

As expected, they didn't text back. They called. Emmaline called first.

"Lacey," she said without preamble. "Please tell me you're not joking because Dora is driving me crazy and I need a break from being a mom like right now." Emmaline had gotten pregnant during our senior year in college and Theodora had arrived shortly after Emmaline turned twenty. They had an unusual relationship, more like sisters than mother and daughter. And that had seemed to be working until recently; Emmaline mentioned on more than one occasion that Theodora was turning into a crazy tween and they barely agreed on anything anymore.

I filled her in and half-way into the call, Misha called as well. I connected the calls. "Don't play with my emotions, Lacey. Please tell me you're serious. I want to be in Vegas like right now. All male revue, baby! Wooohoooo!"

I heard Misha's coworkers cheering in the background. I knew she had me on speakerphone and her entire office was listening. We'd both decided not to go into teaching after being teacher assistants in college and Misha had decided instead to go into interior design. She'd recently started her own interior design firm and it was an open office. No cubicles. Just everyone hanging around designing stuff. Most of her staff were women our age, except for her secretary, who was a sixty-year-old guy who didn't say much. He mostly ignored them and ate BBQ all day. At least, that's what Misha told me. I'd never met the guy.

"No joke. We're going to Vegas ladies."

"Whoop! Whoop!"

"On a private plane..."

"What?" gasped Emmaline.

"And that's not even the best part, all our accommodations are paid for."

"Excuse me!" Misha yelled. "Shut up! You have got to be kidding me." I could hear the ladies in the background asking for more info.

I quickly filled everyone in, barely noticing the challenging trek back to the entrance since I was so excited over the recent turn of events, and when I was done with my story, I was at the gate and my taxi was waiting for me.

"This is crazy," Emmaline said in awe as she digested all the details.

"No, this is awesome," I said with a huge smile on my face as I slid into the taxi, waved good-bye to Peter and thanked God that I hadn't said no to Kadija

3

"Oh my God! I'm in heaven!" Emmaline said, practically falling from the taxi in awe of the building in front of us. Actually, it wasn't simply a building. It was more of a monument to excess and wealth. Apparently, my employer was loaded. I knew he was rich because of the plane, but pastors from megachurches had their own private jets nowadays, so a private plane wasn't as impressive as it used to be.

I didn't realize how rich Oliver actually was until I stood outside his hotel on the strip looking up at it. I stretched my head as far back as possible, but still couldn't see the top of the building. It's as if it extended into another dimension in the sky. It was the tower of Babel, I thought jokingly, as I unloaded our suitcases.

Emmaline was too busy yelling, "Oh my God!" and running around the fountains in awe to help out. I was impressed too. Fountains circled the entrance area, each one grander than the next. I felt as if we were on the set of a movie, a Cinderella remake in the modern world, but we were all going to get our Happily Ever After. But instead of a fairy tale castle, we were in front of a stunning hotel that seemed made for dignitaries and celebrities. I immediately felt out of my element, but before I could focus on my own insecurities, I was distracted by Emmaline who was chatting up the doorman and the valet, it seemed. Apparently, she had no trouble feeling as if she belonged here. She was shaking their hands and introducing herself with a big smile on her face. I bet she was the only guest that had ever expressed an interest in learning the employees' names. They actually seemed a little nervous by all her attention and I could see one of them blushing. And then Emmaline let out one of her signature laughs that drew even more eyes in her direction. I looked at Misha and we smirked.

"You can take the girl out of the country, but you can't take the country out of the girl," she said referring to Emmaline's background which had been similar to my own. Emmaline and I'd been raised in a rural area in Southern Georgia. We'd decided to go off to college in New York together. It had been Emmaline's idea. She'd always been the braver, more outgoing of the two of us.

Misha though was born and raised in Brooklyn and had taken us country bumpkins under her wing. She'd especially been there for Emmaline when she'd become pregnant during our senior year and had thought of quitting school. Misha had arranged for Emmaline to stay with her grandmother in Brooklyn when Emmaline's family had pretty much disowned her for having a baby out of wedlock. It had been tough for Emmaline, but between Misha's help and Emmaline's boyfriend, Colin, things had worked out for the best.

EMMALINE HAD FINISHED college only a semester behind the rest of us and for a while, we thought she would marry Colin. But they'd broken up shortly after senior year and Emmaline refused to talk about it. It was odd. They'd been a great couple and from what Emmaline told me, he was a responsible and loving father who always provided for their daughter and had moved to Florida to be closer to them. Emmaline prided herself on being a super mom and I figured she and Colin probably bumped heads a lot when it came to Theodora. I briefly wondered if Colin was taking care of Theodora while Emmaline took a much-deserved break from mom duty.

Speaking of which, she was definitely not being a mom now as she flirted shamelessly with a group of guys as they exited the hotel. They seemed to be foreign. They were all tall and blonde and regarding Emmaline with amusement and interest as they walked away with regret on their faces.

"See you guys around," Emmaline purred.

Misha laughed as we approached carrying all the baggage, which the doorman quickly took from us, gesturing to another employee to help.

I mumbled a thank you as I said to Emmaline, "Were you trying to flirt with an entire foreign delegation or sports team, whoever they were?"

Misha cut in, "We're only here for the weekend; we have to take advantage of every opportunity."

I shook my head. "You two are something else. And you're married," I said pointedly to Misha.

"But she isn't. She's a single mom who hasn't gotten out of the house in at least a decade. She should be flirting with all the men. ALL."

Misha turned around and headed through the large glass doors held open by the doorman.

Emmaline and I had to come to a sudden halt as we barreled into her solid, unmoving form.

"What—?" I began and then promptly shut my mouth. It was clear what had stopped Misha in her tracks. The gorgeous view in front of us deserved our awe. The inner part of the hotel was just as stunning as the entrance. The hotel was hollow nearly as far as the eye could see, with the rooms on the outer part of the building. A huge sunlight sat in the middle and I stared at it in awe, taking in the ultra-modern and chic decor that reminded me of show homes I saw on television.

I was definitely out of my element, but I was determined not to show it. I squared my shoulders and headed in the direction of the reception desk. A petite brunette greeted us with a warm smile.

"Ms. Cabot, I presume?"

I blinked twice, trying to figure out how she knew my name.

At the confused look on my face, she gave a laugh. "Mr. Oliver mentioned that you were coming."

She busily began to type something into the computer and then looked up again at us with a smile when she was done.

"How was your trip? I heard Oliver's plane is gorgeous."

She called him Oliver. Apparently, she knew my new boss very well.

"Yeah, it was pretty amazing," I said for lack of a better word.

"I heard it had a hot tub," the receptionist said, and I laughed.

"It was amazing, but not THAT amazing."

The receptionist chuckled, reached under the desk and slid over a key card.

"Oh," she said, shaking her head at her error. "You'll need three of these."

She promptly entered something else in the computer, reached under the counter and laid two additional keys next to mine.

"I hope you ladies enjoy your stay. And if you need anything, please feel free to contact me. I'm the concierge here. My name is Renee."

"Thanks, Renee."

She smiled brightly at all of us again and said, "No problem."

We looked around for the guy who had our bags and Renee said, "They're already in your room."

"Oh, wow, now that's impressive," Misha said.

We made our way to the elevators and it promptly opened up. There was a man in uniform inside and I awkwardly stepped in.

"What floor ladies?"

"Umm...." I looked down at our keycard. "Twelve?"

He pushed the button and as the elevator made its way up I could practically feel the excitement in the air. We looked at each other and smiled. The elevator operator noticed and said, "Is this your first time staying at The Xerxes?"

We nodded.

"But you ladies have been to Vegas before, right?"

We all shook our heads and the elevator operator smiled widely, and said, "Tell Renee that. She'll get you set up with the vacation of a lifetime."

He began to tell us about all his favorite shows and sights and before we knew it, we were out of the elevator and heading in the direction of our suite and practically best friends with the elevator operator, Hank.

"See you around, Hank," I called as we made our way.

"He sure was nice," Misha said.

"Yeah, the customer service here has been above reproach," Emmaline added.

We followed the signs that directed us to our room. The floor was padded with luxurious carpet, so thick that you couldn't even hear our footsteps as we made our way towards our room. We easily found it and with bated breath and barely contained excitement, I held up the key card against the lock. There was a little click as I swiped the card, and as I pushed the door open, I gasped.

The room was gorgeous. As I walked in, I noticed that the suite had three separate doors, leading to what I guessed were three separate rooms. We excitedly bounced from room to room, arguing with each other about which room to pick. Not that it mattered, they were all decorated in the same manner: classic, yet modern with understated luxury.

"I can't believe this setup," Emmaline said pulling out her phone and taking a selfie in front of her room. She gestured to the rest of us. "Get in here. Get in close. My kid's going to be soooo jealous."

We did as we were told, making funny faces and laughing the entire time. We located our suitcases in the main living area with the gigantic TV and agreed to meet up downstairs for cocktails or happy hour at one of the restaurants.

As always, I was the first one ready. I was pretty no-nonsense and had changed into a serviceable wrap dress and low heels. I left Misha and Emmaline upstairs changing and decided to explore the hotel a little bit while I waited for them. I found Hank still on duty in the elevator and chatted with him a little more about his favorite places in Vegas until I reached the lobby. I was doing my best to memorize our conversation so that I would have something to share with Emmaline and Misha when they eventually came downstairs.

I looked around the lobby and realized I had quite a few choices in terms of entertainment. I didn't want to seem like a loser sitting by myself doing nothing, so I headed to a restaurant that I'd noticed earlier on. It had seemed pretty laid-back in comparison to the other eateries around me.

The maître d' smiled brightly at me, but the smile didn't reach her eyes, and I pretended that I didn't notice that she didn't seem too impressed with my choice of clothing. I wouldn't have noticed if it weren't for the small frown that marred her face when she saw my shoes, before she caught herself and her forced smile returned. I shrugged it off and raised my chin.

"How many this evening, ma'am?" she said with a slight British accent.

"I thought I'd just sit at the bar, if that's okay."

She seemed relieved. I guess there had to be at least one haughty employee, I thought to myself. I didn't wait for her to say another word. I wanted to be the one who turned my back on her. I made my way to the bar not waiting for her "permission", ignoring the other guests who were dressed as if they were attending the Oscars.

I slid onto a stool and ordered a drink, hoping the ladies wouldn't mind that I started without them.

The bartender slid my drink in front of me. As I said thank you, I noticed someone slide onto the stool next to me. I automatically shifted over, giving the stranger more room than he or she needed, but I figured moving away from the person would dissuade him or her from making idle chitchat with me. I hated chitchat. I didn't want to make eye contact and start a conversation, so I stared studiously down into my glass, hoping that Misha and Emmaline would text me soon.

I thought I heard female voices and looked up in the direction of the entrance. It wasn't them. Disappointed, I turned back to my drink, accidentally glancing in the direction of the stranger. With a sinking feeling, it was then that I noticed the stranger looked familiar. And to my disgust, he sat staring at me with a smile on his face. Unfortunately, I knew that smile and I knew that face.

"Hi, princess," said Jude with a stupid grin. It was actually a beautiful grin, but I didn't want to admit it.

I rolled my eyes in an exaggerated motion and sighed deeply. "What are you doing here, stalker?"

"Oh please, don't pretend you're not thrilled to see me."

"Oh I don't have to pretend anything. I'm absolutely thrilled to see you. I was just thinking to myself, you know what would really make my day: running into my boss's obnoxious son."

He smiled even wider. "So you have been thinking about me. I knew it."

I moved to get up and he watched, taking his time to look at my legs, before bringing his gaze to my breasts.

I planted my hands on my hips, "Seriously. Could you be any more blatant?"

He shrugged and gave me a rakish smile. "You can't blame a man for appreciating the view."

"Well you can appreciate this view as well," I said turning around and marching away from him. I was so angry that I wasn't paying attention to where I was going and ran right smack into the concierge. She looked upset and harried.

"Oh, God. I'm so sorry, miss. Tell me, you wouldn't

have seen a really handsome guy, dark brown eyes, pretty smile somewhere around here, have you?"

"Unfortunately, I have." I gestured towards the bar and the concierge gave me a smile in gratitude before hurrying to Jude's side. It was then that I noticed the phone in her hand. She said something to Jude and then handed him the phone.

Jude looked confused, and I watched as his smile disappeared as he brought the phone to his ear. He caught me looking in his direction, but seemed to look through me as he listened to the voice on the other end, his lips growing tighter as the conversation continued.

Something was clearly wrong, but it was none of my business. I went off to find the girls and didn't have to go far, as they caught up with me as I exited the hotel restaurant.

"Oh, there you are. We were looking everywhere for you..."

I wondered why they stopped talking when abruptly I felt a tap on my shoulder. I turned around already knowing who was there.

"What is it, Jude?"

"We need to talk."

I narrowed my eyes at him, "No way, I'm on vacation. Your dad's orders. And remember, I work for him, not you. Whatever you have to say to me can wait."

"My father's dying."

4

We sat in a meeting space not too far from the restaurant. There were just the two of us and I felt numb. I'd known Oliver was sick, Kadija had hinted at it. I was well aware Oliver wasn't in the best of health, but I'd thought Kadija had been exaggerating once I actually had the opportunity to meet him in person. He'd seemed to be in perfect health and I found myself saying so to Jude.

"I'd heard he wasn't doing great, but I thought it was a gross exaggeration."

Jude laughed bitterly. "Apparently it wasn't."

I didn't know what to say. I'd never been in this predicament. I'd never had to endure through the knowledge that someone close to me was dying. I looked at Jude, studying him. He was turned half away from me, leaning against a wall, just staring out the window with his arms crossed.

He didn't seem upset, just contemplative. He hadn't said much after he dropped the news of his dad's condition. He'd been about to walk off when I'd reached out and stopped him, asking to speak to him alone. Misha and Emmaline had been very accommodating, telling me they'd wait outside for me.

Jude had led me into the conference room, closing the door behind us, not saying much of anything as he stood much like he was now, staring out the window.

I felt I needed to say something. Something reassuring. Something considerate. I really wanted to, but I didn't know how.

I was still struggling to find the words when Jude turned towards me and said, "I don't know about you, but I'm not going to stand here feeling sorry for myself or my father." He laughed bitterly. "I bet that's why he sent me on this bogus trip yesterday. He told me he needed me to check up on The Xerxes personally. I fell for it, thinking he was finally going to let me help out some."

I stayed silent and he shook his head as if to clear it before saying, "He probably knew well before yesterday he was dying. He just wasn't man enough to tell me himself. He left it to his lawyer to tell me. Can you believe that? He sent me out of town on some bogus trip because he couldn't tell me the truth, couldn't tell his own son face-to-face. And his lawyer didn't even call me directly! He called the hotel to reach me and Renee tracked me down. This is ridiculous!" He slammed his fist down on a table and I jumped, startled.

I could hear the pain in his voice and I blinked back tears, not knowing how to react to his anger and underlying sorrow.

Abruptly he said, "I'm sorry. I'm not yelling at you… it's just everything… everything about this situation has me—never mind. I'll see you later, Lacey."

"But—what—we should talk about this," I called after him. "Where are you going?" I grabbed his elbow stopping him from leaving, searched his face for some sort of emotion, but all I saw was resignation and anger. I definitely didn't see sadness anymore.

"Where am I going? I'm going to enjoy my time in Vegas. I'm going to get drunk… and I suggest you do the same."

He left me standing there and sauntered out the door as if he didn't have a care in the world.

I watched him leave, a little taken aback, and then made my way out the conference room. I was accosted by my friends before I even crossed the threshold.

"What happened?" Misha asked, her eyes filled with concern.

I shrugged. "Not sure."

"He looks so familiar. Who is he?" Misha said wondering out loud.

Emmaline chirped, "Ice cream guy? That's him, isn't it?"

I nodded solemnly. "Unfortunately."

I filled them in on my second encounter with Jude on his father's property.

"God, you have the worst luck with first and second impressions, don't you?" asked Misha.

"Yeah that first lunch between you all must have been a little awkward," Emmaline added.

"You have no idea."

"Soooo.... what do you want to do now? I know it must not be the best time to celebrate, but it's still your birthday." Misha was right, but it didn't feel right. I liked Oliver and I was sad that I wouldn't get to know him better, but at the same time, he was mostly a stranger to me.

"I sort of feel guilty thinking about having fun when my employer is apparently dying."

"I understand," Emmaline started. "But from the sound of it, he probably already knew and wanted you to have this as a gift."

Misha chimed in, "I think Emmaline's right."

I knew they were probably right, but I was still a little unsettled. I needed a drink. A stiff one. My employer was dying and I was living it up on his dime for my birthday. It just didn't seem right, but apparently, it was what he wanted.

We headed to a bar not too far from our hotel. It was a pretty classy joint, and I downed more drinks than I should have. I was feeling a little reckless and indecisive and it was easier to pretend to be having a good time than to focus on the bad news I'd just heard. But as the night drew on, I started enjoying myself. I felt so relaxed, so uninhibited and sexy.

I hadn't felt sexy in a long time, I thought to myself as I scanned the crowd, looking for an unattached man to possibly make out with. The girls had been right. I had been through a sex drought since Evan dumped me, and now that I was in Vegas, I was ready for it to end.

I saw a group of men come in, apparently celebrating something. They were a little tipsy and were loud and boisterous, but also not too hot. I figured I had a pretty good chance of picking one of them up.

They began to dance even though it wasn't that type of bar and I found myself laughing at some of their antics.

"You know what, Oliver would want me to live a little. Isn't this what this weekend is about, celebrating life?"

"Exactly," said Emmaline as she focused on something or someone at the door, I looked in that direction but didn't see anyone. I looked at Emmaline curiously and she smiled and shrugged, "I thought I saw someone I recognized."

Abruptly, she stood up and tugged at her mini-skirt that hugged her ample behind. "I'm going to run to the bathroom, be right back." She turned around as she walked away from me and said almost as a second thought, "You should take a chance. It's Vegas after all. And what happens in Vegas stays in Vegas." She winked at me and sashayed off to the bathroom. She was in a fantastic mood. Almost giddy. And she hadn't had one drink. Maybe it was something in the water.

I watched as the men danced around singing, making complete fools of themselves and I found myself standing up, emboldened by the many drinks I'd had.

"Emmaline's right. I need to take a chance, so I'm going to go meet some men." I declared, dusting off my dress. I knew that I looked like a nun who didn't get out much, but I was going to change that. I was going to live life to the fullest and take control of my life like all those memes on the internet suggested.

Misha cheered me on, "Yeah! Girl! Go get them."

I decided to try to be sexy as I approached, spotting one that I felt was just my type. Tall, dorky, wearing a bowling shirt. Oh yeah, he didn't know it yet, but he was getting lucky tonight!

. . .

I DID my best to sashay over to him to the beat of the music, but felt ridiculous as I half bopped and dipped, side-stepped to his side. His friends were turned away, but he watched me with amusement in his eyes.

I didn't care. It was Vegas, right? Who cared what anyone thought? And Evan would be so jealous if he saw me.

"Hey, big boy," I said, trying to sound sexy, leaning against the bar where the guy was suddenly looking nervous and no longer amused. In my drunken state, I thought his nervousness was a good sign.

I attempted to swing my hair in a flirtatious manner over my shoulders and realized that was a wasted effort since I had just gotten my hair cut into a bob not too long ago. My cheeks burned in embarrassment, but I'd come too far to give up now.

"What's a sexy beast like you doing in a dive like this?" My muddled tipsy brain forgot that we were in a classy bar.

He raised an eyebrow. "Sexy beast?"

I placed my hand on my hip. "Obviously I'm not talking about anyone else." I turned until I was facing him and my body was just inches from his. I liked how his glasses were askew and his thin lips formed an unsure, nervous smile. I bet he hadn't had a woman show interest in him in months... maybe even years! Today was his lucky day. Guys like him were my specialty. I loved the rejects because they never rejected me. Well, Evan did, but I was too tipsy to allow my brain to focus on that.

"Listen, buddy. I know I'm a lot of woman to handle, but I'm willing to let you try."

I'd heard that line before in a movie and the woman who had delivered it had sounded pretty sexy. Apparently, I didn't have her same sex appeal. His friends guffawed and I felt my cheeks burning with embarrassment. But, hey, I was supposed to live a little, right? Take some action?

And so I did, I took life by the horns. Or rather, I grabbed his face and pulled it towards mine. He resisted, but apparently being drunk made me stronger. He couldn't get away from me and I kissed him hard and immediately regretted it. He tasted like old beer and even older hamburgers. His eyes were big round saucers as he stared past me, clearly terrified by whatever was behind me.

"What the hell!" yelled someone directly behind me, and I turned only to be greeted by a dark-eyed furious woman who looked more like a teenager than anything else. She had a posse of about five women behind her and they all looked ready to clobber me. I gulped and took a step back.

·   ·   ·

"I'M SORRY—WHO—?"

I didn't get another word out as she punched me hard in my shoulder.

"Ouch! Hey! What's your problem?" I screeched, tearing up a little, more from wounded pride than her blow to my shoulder.

She hit me again and I am embarrassed to admit, I might have whimpered a little bit. I wasn't the physical type, but apparently, she was as she growled, "You're my problem, you home-wrecker. That's my fiancé you had your nasty lips on!"

"Yeah! You whore! Get her, Tanya!" yelled one of her friends. The others echoed their agreement and I quickly put my hands up as if to wave off any future attacks.

I took a few steps back. "Your fiancé?" I heard the guys chuckling in the background and I looked at the fiancé who suddenly seemed unbothered. If anything, he seemed to be enjoying the show. I bet he was just relieved that her anger was directed towards me. I didn't blame him. It was my fault and Tanya was super scary.

"This is my engagement party, you, you, dirty hobag," said Tanya with her fist balled up. I wasn't going to stick around to get punched again and looked around for a quick escape.

"Well then," I chuckled nervously, stepping away from them. "I had no idea." I tried to sneak away, looking in vain for my friends to rescue me, but strangely they were nowhere to be found. Just as I turned away to make a run for it, I felt hands grab me by my hair and the next thing I knew the bride-to-be was wrestling me to the ground.

"Where do you think you're going, you tramp?" she screamed, spittle flying on my face as I tried to knock her off. I pushed at her face with one hand while desperately attempting to roll away. I felt my skirt fly up and the snickering from the guys with the laughs from the women made me want to just give up and let Tanya kill me.

But self-preservation won out and I kicked at her, sending her sprawling backward. My legs felt like Jell-O but I tried to crawl away as fast as possible, panting as I crawled between the legs of one of her friends.

"Hey!" she called out as I practically mowed her over. Just as I thought I was reaching freedom, Tanya caught me by my legs and I went sprawling to my tummy, screaming and trying to grab hold to any legs I could as she dragged me away.

"Help! Somebody! Anybody! Help!" I cried as I managed to flip over and disentangle one foot from her grasp. Valiantly with the other, I kicked at her.

"Tanya! Don't kill me! Please! Please! Don't kill me!" I found myself begging. By now, what felt like the whole bar was gathered around like this was some sort of

UFC/MMA fight. If Tanya didn't kill me, embarrassment sure would.

Tanya tossed herself on top of me and sitting on my belly began to slap me. Yelling out, "Whore, tramp," and a variety of other colorful phrases.

Over my whimpering and crying, I heard someone yelling, "Break it up. Come on, break it up." And then miraculously the weight of Tanya's body was no longer on my abdomen and someone was reaching for my hand trying to pull me up.

I grasped hold of the hand and dared to open my eyes. To my surprise, it was Jude. I hugged his neck, "Oh thank God. You saved me. These people are monsters!"

Tanya was being held back by her fiancé as she growled and lunged at me, I screeched and hid behind Jude.

"She's sorry. We're sorry. Excuse us." Jude said pushing me quickly toward the exit. I glanced behind me and saw that Tanya had escaped her fiancé's grasp and was still coming after me.

"Oh my God. She's like the Terminator. Run, Jude! Run!"

He seemed to find my words amusing until he looked behind us and saw Tanya's murderous face. He pushed past me, yelling, "Let's go! She's possessed! Come on, Lacey!"

We pushed through the exit and raced down the

street, Jude ahead, me limping behind him, until finally we saw another bar and disappeared into it. We collapsed against the side of the bar, trying to catch our breath.

"Now that—" I started.

"Was humiliating," he finished.

Our eyes met and we started to laugh. My ribs hurt, my face hurt, and I was pretty sure I looked like a wild monster, but I couldn't help but find the situation so ridiculous that it was actually amusing.

Jude's laugh was contagious. It was a deep belly laugh, so un-self-conscious and genuine. We must have looked like two crazy people, laughing hysterically.

Our laughter died down and Jude stared at me. I knew I must have looked a mess and I was sure I was covered in dirt and scratches.

And then Jude surprised me by beginning to laugh even harder.

I turned bright red. "I know... I know… I must look..." I stopped talking as I caught a look at myself in the mirror directly across from us. My wrap dress had come undone and you could see everything. And I mean, everything. I gasped as I tried to right my dress, spinning around in a circle trying to find the other part of my dress.

"Oh god oh god," I said over and over and Jude's

laughter grew louder, drawing even more looks and a few giggles.

I hit him in a fit of despair and desperation. "Stop laughing, you… you… juvenile man-boy and help me!"

He did as he was told with a stupid grin on his face the whole time. He handed me the other half of my dress and I quickly wrapped it back in the front and tied the belt in a knot.

"Thank you," I muttered, unjustifiably angry with him although this had been the second time he'd saved me that evening. When did I become the damsel in distress type?

"Can I ask you a question?" he said, once I righted myself.

"No." I was being contrary and stubborn because I was embarrassed.

"Okay, I'm going to pretend you said yes. What the hell happened back there?"

I folded my arms across my chest and spoke with a voice full of indignation, as if I was the one who had been wronged as I answered, "I was accosted by that woman. You saw what happened."

"Umm yeah, I saw that part. Now that was a sight… but what started the catfight?"

"Catfight? How sexist!"

"Okay then, let me rephrase, what caused her to kick your ass up and down the bar floor? Literally."

I felt myself blushing. "It was just a misunder-standing."

"A misunderstanding?" He had a wicked gleam in his eyes and I felt as if he were already mocking me.

"Yes, a misunderstanding. Nothing more. Nothing less."

"So it had nothing to do with anything? She was just a random crazy person who attacked you?"

"Yep," I lied running a nervous hand through my hair and finding scraps of debris and an entire cashew. I flung it over my shoulder.

"I could have eaten that," Jude said faking sadness.

"You're so gross."

"That might be true, but at least I'm not the one trying to pick up almost married dudes the day before their wedding."

I wanted the ground to open up right then and there and swallow me.

"Oh gosh, was it that obvious?"

"Umm yeah. It was clearly an engagement party."

"So you were there the whole time?" I said feeling lower than low. "Then why'd you ask me what happened?"

He shrugged. "I just wanted to see if you'd own up to it. And you didn't. Figured as much."

"So you saw me when I—"

"Walked up to the poor guy and glued your mouth to

him... yep, that was... interesting. Didn't figure you for the type."

"What type?" I said in a dark voice.

He wisely changed the subject. "So why him? Out of all the guys in the bar?"

Without thinking, I said, "It wasn't my fault. He just, you know looked like the type who would be single."

"What?" Jude laughed dryly. "That's just mean. Ouch. So harsh. So perpetually single guys have a certain look?"

I blushed, feeling bad. "No, I just mean, that he wasn't exactly the most attractive guy in the building—" I shut myself up. I was definitely putting my foot in my mouth.

"So that's your mode of operation? You pick the most unattractive dude out of the bunch and stick your tongue down his throat. If that's the case, it's no wonder you're still single."

"What's that supposed to mean?" I narrowed my eyes at him. "And what makes you think I'm single?"

"I heard your little conversation at the ice cream shop, remember?"

At that moment, I wanted to clobber my friends like Tanya had clobbered me.

I groaned, "How about we just forget all that and call it a night, shall we? Good night, Jude."

I walked away from him but didn't get very far. He

caught me by my elbow and turned me around. "You owe me a drink."

"Excuse me?" I pulled my elbow from his grasp.

"I was happily drinking some really good beer before I had to abandon it to save you."

"One less beer won't kill you. Goodnight Jude."

"Come on, Lace."

"It's Lacey," I hissed. "And I need to get back to my friends."

"Just text them... tell them you'll catch up with them later. Please."

I was ready to walk away, but something about the way he called me Lace instead of Lacey, the familiarity of his words and his tone, which showed a hint of underlying sadness made me hesitate.

I looked into Jude's eyes then and realized Jude wasn't drinking for fun. Jude was in pain. He just did a very good job at hiding it. And part of me didn't want the craziness of this night to end. Despite the girl fight, I was actually having a good night, but clearly Jude wasn't.

"You're worried about your father, aren't you?"

He shrugged, trying to come across as nonchalant, "Aren't you?"

I didn't get a chance to answer as he cut into my next words. "Come on, Lacey, have a drink with me. You don't even have to buy them. I'll pay."

"You should, you're the rich one."

"So that's a yes, then?"

I wanted to say no, I truly did. The last thing I needed was to sit around drinking with my employer's son. But a drink or two wouldn't hurt anyone, right? Especially a drink with an attractive man. I immediately shoved the thought to the back of my mind and he lent me his phone to text the girls. In my haste to get away from Tanya, I'd left my purse with my cellphone behind.

I quickly texted Misha and Emmaline and handed Jude back his phone. He slid it into his pocket.

"Shall we?"

I let him lead me to the bar and after we ordered our drinks, I gave him a stern glance, "One drink. That's all."

"No problem."

"And no funny business," I warned, pointing my finger at him as if I were a kindergarten teacher scolding a student.

"Cross my heart. I promise to be on my best behavior, but you're one to talk... I didn't single-handedly break up an engagement party by kissing the groom."

"Soon-to-be groom," I grumbled.

Jude laughed, "Maybe. If Tanya didn't turn her rage on him after we left..."

"Ran. We ran."

Jude looked offended. "I only ran because you ran."

I giggled. "Your eyes were wide in fear when Tanya was chasing behind us."

JUDE SHRUGGED. "She was one scary bridezilla. But enough about Tanya." He picked up the drinks the bartender had left for us. He handed one to me and took the other.

"What should we drink to?"

I shrugged. "World peace?"

Jude looked at me in disgust. "We're in Vegas, Lacey. Come on."

Annoyed and feeling judged for being a stick-in-the-mud, I said, "Well then you choose, Jude."

He studied me and his eyes lingered on the top of my breasts which I realized were on display courtesy of Tanya who had damaged my dress beyond function. I clumsily tried to adjust it and cleared my throat, signaling Jude to just make his damn toast.

"To Lacey, a woman who never shies away from a fight." I smiled until he continued, "And to Lacey's dress, may it continue to fall apart at the seams, because I definitely like seeing what's underneath."

My mouth was wide open as he smiled wickedly at me and clinked his glass against mine.

My head was killing me. That was my first thought as my body reluctantly stirred into consciousness. I'd been having the weirdest dream, actually, the sexiest dream. I'd been arguing with Jude. About what, I wasn't too sure, but our argument had ended with us having sex up against a wall. And it had been delicious. I couldn't remember any other details, but I knew it'd been good. Real good.

But my reality was far from good. I groaned as I attempted to sit up and told myself that I'd never drink again. The room began to spin because my head hurt so badly, and I collapsed back down onto the pillows letting out a long sigh. I closed my eyes, willing the sunlight that peeked through the blinds to go away. I was far too weak to deal with life today and my head felt like it would fall off. *Perhaps I'll just stay here... forever.*

I opened my eyes and looked around. I blinked once and then again. Where the heck was I? I closed my eyes, counted to ten and then opened them again, assuming that I was dreaming. I was definitely not in my hotel room. I had no clue where I was and I forced myself not to panic.

"Ugggghhhhhhh."

My body went still and all thoughts about controlling my panic disappeared as fear took over. I was fairly confident that I wasn't the one who had groaned unless the hangover I was experiencing was making me hallucinate.

"Ughhhhhhhh…" came the noise again. And this time I was sure it wasn't me. *Oh God, I'd been kidnapped and my kidnapper was coming for me!*

With all the strength I could muster, I tossed myself off the bed and hit the floor with a thud. I tried to hide myself by rolling under the bed, but realized I wouldn't ever fit with my gigantic butt.

I heard the groan again. In panic, I reached for the first thing my hand landed on. A shoe. Armed with it, I crawled around the bed, trying to be quiet, ignoring the pounding headache. I could see the door from where I was positioned and I made a quick decision to leave the crouching position I was currently in.

I jumped up with the shoe and ran to the door, only realizing as I was about to open it that I was completely naked except for the sheet that was wrapped around me.

I heard the groaning again and realized someone was in the bed I'd just left. I wasn't stopping to find out who it was, so with shaky hands, I pried open the lock and deadbolt and made a dash for the hallway.

I ran as fast as I could and I heard someone yell from behind me, "Hey!"

I didn't turn around. I wasn't interested. Luckily the elevators were at the end of the hall, and I hit both buttons, not caring if it took me up or down.

"Lacey! Wait!" A voice called out for me and I looked back, not expecting the sight that greeted me—Jude completely naked standing in the hall with his hands on his hips looking confused and annoyed.

My mouth opened and then closed. I didn't know what to say. I didn't know what to do. And before I could figure out my next course of action, the elevator opened and I stepped on, wrapping my sheet as close to my body as possible.

"Where are you—"

He didn't get another word out as the elevator doors closed and I breathed a sigh of relief. Apparently, I hadn't been kidnapped. I hadn't been in danger, but I had indeed made a very, very bad decision.

It took me a few minutes before I remembered I was in my hotel. Or should I say, Oliver Foster's hotel.

I stepped into the lobby, more concerned that a naked Jude would follow me there than the fact that I was walking around like a crazy woman with one shoe in her hand and wearing a sheet as a dress. I'd done my best to make it look like a toga while I was in the elevator, but given the amount of space everyone who got into the elevator gave me, I was guessing my makeshift toga wasn't very convincing.

I took a look around trying to get my bearings and not freak out when a warm voice said, "Good morning, Lacey."

It was the concierge, Renee. I felt my cheeks turn red. I was probably bruised from my fight with Tanya. I was wearing a sheet. I was dirty. I was carrying one shoe. I looked at it, like really looked at it for the first time. At least it was my own, I thought with a sigh.

"Are you okay?" Renee asked me as she looked at my sheet wrapped body.

"Fine. Dandy. I'm just going to make my way back upstairs...." I tried to make small talk as I stood there and waited for the elevator to come back down.

"So I guess Hank has the day off?"

She shook her head. "He'll be in later. He had car trouble. Are you sure there's nothing I can do for you?" I felt so bad. She looked so concerned, but what was I supposed to say? Keep naked Jude away from me?

"Uhhh... no, everything's fine. I just lost my shoe.

Thought I might have left it downstairs," I lied unconvincingly.

Renee gave me one last look, a small confused smile and then walked away. Finally, the elevator binged and I climbed on, thankful that I would finally escape to my room when a hand reached out and caught the elevator stopping it.

I sighed in frustration. Great, another person to witness my humiliation. In vain, I tried to adjust the sheet that was pooling around my ankles and prepared myself emotionally for the uncomfortable stares I was sure I would get.

To my surprise, it was Hank. He was kind enough to pretend he didn't notice my strange attire. We chatted about nothing and I was so grateful when we reached my floor.

As I walked out, I dropped my shoe and he graciously recovered it for me saying with a wink, "Don't worry, miss. What happens in Vegas—"

"Stays in Vegas. Thanks for the reminder, Hank."

I waved bye and hurriedly made my way to my room. I knew from talking to Hank that it was still really early, not yet 7 in the morning. I just wanted to sneak back into my room before the girls woke up and saw me.

I knew I'd get lots of questions, but I couldn't face

them like this. This was worse than the walk of shame. This was like the marathon of shame.

I got to the door and realized with a sinking heart that I didn't have my key. Resigned, I knocked and then knocked again. I waited a few minutes and when no one showed up, I knocked again harder.

I heard the sound of the chain being removed from the door and sighed in relief as the door opened.

"Thank you," I said to Misha who didn't look in the least concerned that I was standing in the hallway wrapped in a sheet.

"I can explain."

"You don't need to. I already did," came a voice from inside. I knew that voice and I felt my head pounding at the sound of it. Or maybe that was the hangover. I didn't know.

"Jude," I said shortly, trying to muster some dignity as I stuck my nose in the air haughtily. "What are you doing here?"

He was standing in the living room of our hotel suite, relaxed and handsome. And of course, well put together. It pissed me off that I was the one looking like an escapee from an insane asylum and he looked like a young version of Patrick Dempsey.

"I'm just returning this," he said, holding up my shoe. "I guess you left it in your haste, Cinderella."

His tone was mocking and I wanted to punch him. I

refrained. I'd been in enough fights in Vegas. I didn't need to lose another one.

I walked over to him as gracefully as I could. I heard a noise from Misha and realized that she was trying to cover up a giggle. I shot her a cold look and she promptly exploded in giggles.

My lips tightened and I moved to snatch the shoe from Jude's hands. He pulled his hand back at the last minute and said, "Hey, no snatching. Play nice. I'm sure you were raised better than that."

I rolled my eyes and snatched the shoe out of his hand. "Thanks. Now go."

"We need to talk," he said trailing behind me as I made my way to my room.

"We have nothing to talk about..."

I then shot a glare at Misha, "I can't believe you let him in."

Her eyes grew wide in disbelief and she said pointedly, "I can't believe you let him in... either... if you know what I mean."

"Nice, Misha. Real mature," I said, knowing I was misdirecting my anger. She wasn't the one I was mad at. No, only Jude deserved my indignation and anger, so I turned on him.

I poked him in the chest with my finger. "You need to leave right now! I've had enough of you and your shenanigans. Ever since I met you I've gotten into one stupid situation after another and you know what the common denominator is?"

"Uhh—"

"You!" I said, poking him with more force. "I wish I hadn't said yes to your father, because it's been one nightmare after another."

"And I'm to blame for that? I've spent the last 24 hours saving you from yourself."

"You're an asshole."

"And you're a hypocrite. You pretend to be all respectable and saintly, when you're just like the rest of us... except you're undersexed and uptight. Well, not anymore. Not after last night."

I smacked him across the chest with one of the shoes. "How dare you judge me! You don't even know me. You're just a spoiled rich boy with too much time on his hands. I mean look at you, your father is dying and where are you? Here! In Vegas! Partying! Preying on innocent women—"

"Innocent?" he spat out. "You're far from innocent. You had your hands down my pants before we even left the bar."

"Liar!" I yelled, but instantly felt guilty. He was right. As soon as he said it I remembered doing it.

"Stop being a prude," he said hotly. "God, I like you better when you're drunk."

"I can barely stomach you when I'm sober so I'm sure drunk me was a real peach."

"You're less of a drab, self-pitying shrew when you're drunk."

God, I wanted to hit him again.

"Pity? You want to talk about pity? I only had drinks with you because I pitied you. I said to myself, 'What type of guy goes to Vegas alone and follows his dad's assistant around?' A loser, that's who," I said, stomping further into my room. I tried to close the door and he caught it. He looked angry. I determinedly didn't back down from his glare and met it head on.

"Oh, that's rich, so I'm the loser? That makes me just your type then. That's your specialty, losers, right? Date a loser to make yourself feel better so that you don't have to deal with your own shortcomings and insecurities. When are you going to stop being a scared little girl and grow up?"

"You're one to talk, a washed-up soccer player living off of daddy's money, too busy whoring to hold down a real job. Yeah, you're definitely one to talk."

"That's what you think of me?"

"Wrong. I don't think about you at all."

"Funny, that's not what you said last night."

Bits and pieces of our night together between the sheets flashed across my mind. I felt embarrassment starting to replace my anger, but I needed my anger, otherwise Jude would know just how much last night's events had unnerved me.

"Last night I was drunk. You got me drunk." My accusation was false. I remembered ordering more and more drinks at the bar. It had all been my doing and I remember distinctly that Jude had told me to slow down and I had scoffed at him and yelled, "We're in Vegas, baby!"

He called me out on my lie. "That's bull and you know it."

Angrily, I tried to shut the door again and he caught it.

"Just leave me alone!"

"Trust me, Lacey, I would love to, but we need to talk."

"I have nothing to say to you. And I don't want to hear anything you have to say to me." I was ready to cry and I needed him to go away. I wanted to be alone with my feelings. I couldn't handle being around him now. And so in a last ditch effort, I got mean.

"Get out. I don't want to see you again. I made a mistake. I felt sorry for you so I made a mistake. Leave me alone."

"Sorry for me, huh?" I could hear the hurt in his voice, but I couldn't back down now. Apparently, I didn't need to. He was done fighting with me.

Without another word, he turned around and

walked away, tossing something down on the chair as he did. He disappeared through the door and I breathed a sigh of relief.

"That was painful to watch. Why were you so mean? It was just a one-night stand. Been there, done that." Misha said picking up whatever Jude had tossed down.

I ignored her question and asked about Emmaline. "She's not up yet? She's normally up before us."

"She had a late night too. You two losers pretty much ditched me at the same time. I caught a taxi and sat here and ate chocolate all night. You guys made me feel so good about myself..." her voice trailed off as she turned her attention to the papers in her hand.

"Late night? Seriously... like with a man?" I was surprised. As far as I knew, Emmaline hadn't dated anyone since Colin.

Misha didn't answer and instead seemed to be focused on whatever was in her hand. "Umm... you might need to sit down for this."

"What is it?" I asked warily. Something about her tone made me reluctant to learn the answer.

I sat down next to her and realized she was holding photos. I peered closer and realized that they were pictures of me and Jude.

And Jude had been right, I had been all over him, as he smiled widely into the camera. I looked so happy. I was smiling in some of the pics, kissing him in others and then in the last pic, I was beaming as I held up my hand to the camera.

Something about my hand was different. I stared at the pic, not understanding what I saw there. And then my lack of understanding turned into disbelief. I was wearing a ring. I didn't wear rings and the ring on my finger in the picture was not just any type of ring; it was clearly a wedding band.

"Misha?" I said. "Please tell me that's not a ring."

She was staring at my hand now. "That's definitely a ring. Same ring you were wearing in the picture. It looks like a wedding band, Lacey."

I swallowed hard and removed the ring. "Misha? What did I do?"

"This," she said handing me the last remaining paper in her hand.

I studied it for a second, looked around for a garbage can, and promptly threw up.

6

I paced back and forth. I didn't even know why I was pacing. I then started chewing on my lip and mumbling to myself.

"Lacey, are you okay?" asked Emmaline, staring at me funny.

"I'm fine. Perfect. Thanks." I didn't stop pacing.

"You need to sit down. You don't look so good."

"I'm fine. I just need to figure this out. Everything will be fine." I didn't believe my own words but I was desperately trying to not freak out. In fact, I was a second away from freaking out. Suddenly the room was spinning and I struggled to stay standing up as I felt hands assisting me into a sitting position.

"It's okay, Lacey. We got you. Take a deep breath."

I tried to do as they said, but I was gulping air in the

midst of a full-blown panic attack. Married! I couldn't be married! What was wrong with me?

I felt my friends pushing my head between my legs, telling me to breathe.

I focused on their words, gasping for air at first until finally, I was able to take a breath without feeling as if it were a challenge.

I slowly raised my head and looked at them. "I'm okay. Thanks. I was just—well, I don't know—"

I tried to shrug it off and looked at my friends whose eyes were full of concern. I instantly felt embarrassed for losing it for a second. I had to get my emotions under control. I straightened my shoulders, stiffened my spine and declared, "I'm going to get an annulment. That's clearly the only thing to do from here."

Misha and Emmaline nodded silently.

"Okay. I'm going to go find Jude. I'm sure he'll agree to it."

Emmaline nodded in encouragement, but Misha for some reason looked doubtful.

"What?" I asked, not understanding her look.

She said with hesitation in her voice, "It's just that he didn't seem to be too upset by this whole issue. When he was here, he was so calm, he didn't tell me why he was here, just that he wanted to speak to you, but I think he might actually be taking the news better than you..."

"So what are you saying?" My mind jumped to the

most obvious conclusion. "You think he set this up? He did this on purpose?"

"What? No! I mean, I don't know why he would. Why would he do something like that?"

I shook my head, "Yeah. I don't know. I just—I'm not thinking right. I need to go to talk to him." I stood up and promptly headed to the door when I realized I still wasn't wearing much.

"I'll change my clothes first."

"Why are you wearing a sheet, by the way?" Emmaline asked, having only heard part of the story since she had woken up shortly after Jude left.

I opened my mouth and then closed it.

"I'll catch Emmaline up on last night's events, you get changed."

I thanked Misha, trying to ignore the blush creeping up on my cheeks as Misha began explaining the whole sordid tale to Emmaline.

I hurriedly tossed a shirt and jeans on. I ran a hand through my hair and brushed my teeth. I splashed water on my face and gave myself a pep talk.

"You're going to go over there and demand an annulment immediately. Don't get distracted by his bedroom eyes. Or his sexy body. Or his beautiful smile. Or the way he smells, and his skin..." Oh God, I was in trouble.

With purpose in my steps, I strode past my friends, determined to expediently get done what needed to be done. I got on the elevator and realized that I had no clue where I was going. I turned to Hank who looked at me questioningly and said, "Hank, you wouldn't happen to know what floor Jude Foster is on, would you? I swear I'm not trying to stalk him. I work for his dad and I—"

"No need to explain." He selected a floor and we rode in awkward silence. I think I was the only one feeling awkward.

"Would you happen to know his room number?"

Hank laughed. "He owns the whole floor. His is the only place here. Go ahead and knock, I'm pretty sure he's in."

I thanked Hank and made my way to Jude's door. I didn't know what I was going to say, but I hoped Jude wouldn't close the door in my face once he saw me. I'd been mean and nasty, and I was ashamed of how I had reacted.

It wasn't his fault I'd got drunk. It wasn't his fault that we'd got married. None of it was 100% his fault. I just hated that I'd let myself lose control to the point where I made the biggest mistake of my life.

I mustered up some courage and knocked lightly on Jude's door as if I actually didn't want him to answer. I waited for a second and then raised my hand to knock again, when Jude pulled the door open.

He didn't look happy to see me.

"What can I do for you, Lacey?" His words were friendly enough, polite obviously, but his face was unsmiling. He didn't look like his normal gregarious, anything-goes self. He looked serious, no nonsense. I wasn't used to this version of Jude.

Softly I said, "Can we talk?"

"Talk? I thought we didn't have anything to talk about."

"I was wrong," I said with a shrug.

He didn't respond. He stepped back, and with a sweeping arm gesture invited me in. Reluctantly I crossed the threshold, secretly afraid that once I stepped in I'd see hints of our indiscretion.

Bits and pieces of last night were coming back to me and I avoided looking at his coffee table where our indiscretion had started. And I equally avoided looking towards the bedroom door where our indiscretion had ended.

I avoided his eyes and looked anywhere else. My gaze settled on a pile of clothes I realized were mine. He saw me looking and said something about dropping them off downstairs with Renee for me.

His tone was nonchalant, but I knew he was making idle chitchat. He clearly didn't want to have this conversation either, so I cut to the chase.

"What are we going to do?"

Jude took his time answering as he moved to his

couch and sat down. He crossed one ankle over the other and folded his arms behind his head. The position emphasized his muscular arms which I remembered the feel of, and his long legs stretched out in front of him made me remember the feel of his strong thighs under mine as I rode him last night.

I didn't like the direction of my thoughts and apparently, I'd spent too long staring at Jude, speechless. He easily figured out where my thoughts had gone, saying, "Your memory's coming back now, huh?"

It seemed pointless to play coy and I just answered honestly. "Unfortunately."

He laughed, that playful expression that I remembered all too well back in his eyes. I didn't want to admit I was glad to see him smile. I missed his smile.

"I know I was drunk, but I wasn't that bad, was I?"

"I'm not here to stroke your ego."

"Are you here to stroke something else?"

I rolled my eyes. "Can you be serious for one moment?"

"Yeah, but that moment passed. Come sit down. I don't bite... Mrs. Foster." He gestured for me to sit down next to him and instead I sat in the accent chair across from him.

"About this Mrs. Foster thing, how soon can we get an annulment?"

He laughed bitterly. "You want the bad news or the good news first?"

Impatiently, I said, "Just spit it out."

He nodded and folded his hands together and leaned forward. He put his face in his hands and rubbed hard, as if trying to build up to say something he'd regret.

"Come on, Jude. You're killing me here."

"So I called my dad's lawyer. And apparently, the guy can't keep his mouth shut."

"What? What happened?" I didn't understand what he was talking about.

"I called to see about an annulment..."

"And?"

"It's possible."

"Thank God," I breathed.

"But it means I'll lose everything."

"What? Lose everything? What are you talking about?" I didn't like this turn of events.

"Apparently, as soon as dad's lawyer found out, he told my dad who promptly changed not only his will but the stipulations of my inheritance as well. I was supposed to receive the first part of my trust fund on my thirtieth birthday which is in six months, but now our 'situation' has changed things."

I shook my head, not understanding, "So what does that mean? What's going on? I don't understand."

"That means, Lacey, that if we divorce I lose my trust

fund. Dad thinks that by being married, especially to you, I'll learn something about responsibility and maturity before I inherit a giant chunk of money."

"Well, that's wishful thinking. Delusional even. You don't even know what the word maturity means."

"Touché."

I decided to stop giving him a hard time and said, "I mean, that sucks, but that has nothing to do with me."

Jude laughed, "You really don't spare any feelings, do you?"

"I can be a little blunt. But you'll have to forgive me for not caring that you'll have to just be like the rest of us and find a job."

"I have a job—"

"Being a billionaire playboy is not a job."

"I'm not going to argue with you." He now seemed majorly annoyed.

"Good because you'll just lose."

"Do you have to be right all the time?" he asked testily.

"It's what I'm good at."

He smiled gently and said in a soft voice, "I don't know. I remember a few details from last night and you're good at a lot of things."

From the tone of his voice and the wicked gleam in his eyes, I knew "a lot of things" was sexual in nature.

I folded my arms over my chest, pretending to be

more upset than I actually was. Inside I was secretly cheering for making an impression on a man who probably had slept with hundreds of girls, movies stars, models, and he was impressed by my moves? I wanted to pat myself on the back. And then I felt stupid and quickly squashed my reaction to his compliment.

"That may be true, but you'll never get that experience again. You'll just have your memories to sustain you."

He laughed and as he did, something near my foot caught his eye.

He got up and bent down next to me. "I was wondering where these had gone."

To my embarrassment, he was holding my panties from last night.

"Give me those!" I demanded, holding my hand out.

He extended them, I grabbed for them but before my hand clasped around them, he pulled them back. I stood up and placed my hand on my hips and glared at him.

"Stop being such a child."

"I can't, it's in my nature." He gave me a stupid smile that I'm ashamed to admit made me want to drop my panties again. The panties I was wearing.

"Say please."

"Huh?" I said distracted by the direction of my own thoughts.

"If you want them back, say please."

"No way. They're rightfully mine. Give them back."

I moved to grab them and he caught my hand in his. He surprised me then as he wound his fingers through mine and pulled me close.

"What are you doing?" I asked softly. I knew my voice betrayed my excitement at being so close to him.

He settled my body against his, but didn't release me. I looked at our hands wound together. And I realized then that he was still wearing his wedding band. Why hadn't he taken it off?

Something about the realization stirred my heart. I looked into his eyes and said, "You forgot to take your ring off."

"So you noticed? I'm not surprised. You notice everything." He released my hand and traced the side of my face, catching me off guard. It was a tender gesture, not even remotely sexual, but I was turned on by it. That realization made my logical self want to flee, but my legs were glued to that spot as my eyes locked with his.

Desire.

I could see it in his eyes, feel the heat emanating off his body. And I knew as he made eye contact with me he wasn't faking it. He wanted me. He wanted me bad. And I wanted him too.

He pressed his mouth against mine. He kissed me deeply, never letting go of my face. His lips were gentle as he parted mine with his own, letting his tongue take its time to explore my mouth.

I sighed against him, loving the feel of his warm hands against my face as he kissed me. I couldn't help myself as I brought my hands up to his chest, digging my nails into his shirt. Then I encircled his neck with my arms, pressing my breasts against his shirt, trying my best to get closer to him, needing to feel his body pressed against mine.

He broke the kiss to look down between us, and I could feel his manhood pressing against the inside of my thigh. He met my eyes as if asking for permission.

"What are you waiting for?" was my answer.

He picked me up then and I wrapped my legs around his waist. He carried me into the bedroom and placed me down on the bed.

He didn't hurry as he undressed me. And I wasn't in any hurry to stop him. I wanted this. If I was truthful with myself, I'd wanted him since I'd laid eyes on him in the restaurant.

He pulled off my jeans and tossed them to the side. He made short work of the rest of my clothes, ridding me of my bra but keeping my panties on.

I didn't shy away from his gaze. I liked the way he looked at me. He studied me as if he were trying to memorize every part of me. His gaze made me feel beautiful and wanted.

He began to unbutton his shirt, but I couldn't wait that long to touch him again. I sat up and helped him, sliding my hands over his warm, heavily muscled body. I pushed his shirt down his broad shoulders, marveling at how chiseled and perfect he was. I started at his pants, unbuttoning them and pushing them down his legs. He stood up and in one smooth motion, let his pants and boxers fall to the floor.

I reached for his sex, stroking it boldly as it pulsated in my hands. I leaned down to take it in my mouth but he didn't let me.

Instead, he pushed me back against the bed and covered my body with his own. He didn't waste any time, pulling one of my nipples into his mouth while roughly squeezing the other one.

"Jude," I gasped.

He abruptly stopped and started planting kisses between my breasts, making his way downwards. His warm mouth against my skin triggered sensation after glorious sensation.

He continued planting kisses on my belly, until he was kneeling between my knees. He parted my thighs with his hands and began placing kisses there as well. I gasped, as he neared my femininity and tried not to scream as his tongue began tracing circles around my clit through the fabric of my panties.

I was wet and shaking as he grabbed my hips in his

hands and pulled my body closer to his face, pushing my panties to the side, lowering his mouth to my sex as he alternated between kissing my clit and licking my folds. I spread my legs wider and grabbed his head, threading my fingers through his hair as my hips rose up and down, rubbing my sex against his mouth, his tongue.

He ripped my panties off and flung the fabric across the room. He thrust his tongue into me then, licking at my wetness, playing with my clit. What his lips couldn't reach, his tongue sure did, and I rode his face with wild abandonment, gasping his name.

He thrust a finger into me, and my body tensed as I began to come. My insides gripped his finger, and he pushed it in deeper, before pulling it out slowly and licking my juices.

"Turn over," he ordered. With shaking legs, I did as I was told.

I felt him behind me as I stretched my arms out in front of me, grabbing at the sheets in anticipation of what was coming. He was pressed against my bare butt, and he placed his hands around my waist, pulling me back to where he wanted me.

With one hand, he opened my folds, and I felt him slowly push inch by inch inside of me. I buried my face in the sheets, fighting back a moan as he filled me, stretched me.

It hurt a little, and I realized I was probably still sore

from last night's happenings. All thoughts ceased as he moved inside me, gently at first and then he began to speed up.

"Don't stop," I groaned.

He responded by pushing deeper into me, while bringing a hand in between my legs and stroking my clit.

"Jude, oh, Jude."

"You want more?"

"Yes—" I gasped as this time he shoved into me with more force and I struggled to handle him. I wiggled my hips and attempted to spread my legs wider. He felt... bigger.

He kept pushing into me, pulling out and then thrusting in deeply. I couldn't help it, I began to come. The feel of his thickness filling me, spreading me wider, sent pleasure radiating from my center, and I started to scream. The pleasure intensified as he continued to rub my clit with every thrust.

My sex quivered and tightened around his.

"Juuudddeee," I moaned.

"Come for me, baby," he said, and I did. Hard. I was gasping for breath, shaking all over, so wet, so spent. My thighs shook, my breathing was heavy and I could only lie there in the aftermath of my orgasm as he came inside me, groaning, burying himself deeply into me as he grabbed my breasts.

My nipples were hard in his hands and even as he came I felt myself getting turned on again.

"Already?" Jude asked with a laugh.

"Shut up and fuck me, Jude."

Without pause, he responded, "Yes, ma'am."

I tossed my arm over my eyes. Oh God, Lacey, what did you do? What did you do? And the sad part was that I couldn't even blame drunkenness this time. It was straight up bad judgment and horniness.

I gingerly stood up and looked for my clothes. I tried to rehearse what I would say to Jude. I felt torn between either sneaking out like a guilty person or making a scene in which I blamed him for my bad judgment.

I made my way out of his bedroom and found him sitting on the couch, his back to me with his phone in his hand. He didn't hear me behind him, his phone had his undivided attention.

I looked over his shoulder to see what he was looking at. I was surprised, so surprised that I guess I must have made a sound.

He looked up at me and smiled wanly. "That expression on your face was exactly like mine when I found these on my phone."

He showed me a series of selfies of us looking happy and ridiculous. We were posing with Elvis who I assumed officiated our ceremony. I felt sick to my stomach, not because I'd done something so insanely stupid but because I'd never seen myself look happier than the moments caught in those pictures. I looked so carefree, so sure of myself, so happy. And it made me sad to think the inebriated version of myself was the daring, happy one, while sober me was dull and too scared to take chances. Well, I thought guiltily, both versions of me apparently liked having sex with Jude way too much.

"While you were napping I spoke to my dad's lawyer again. I tried to reason with them, but apparently they're beyond reason," Jude said breaking me away from my thoughts. "So Lacey, I have a proposition for you."

I sat down and tried to look receptive. I didn't think I wanted to hear his proposition, but I tried to keep an open mind, meanwhile, I shut him down in my head.

"I propose we stay married—"

"You're insane!" I was suddenly standing up.

"Calm down, calm down, just hear me out," he said, standing up as well. His brown eyes looked slightly offended.

"No—"

"Lacey, I'm begging you. Just sit down. Let's have a conversation like reasonable adults. We've done enough arguing and bad decision-making for a lifetime in a span of twenty-four hours. Will it really hurt any to just have a discussion?"

He had a point. I grudgingly sat down, folded my arms across my chest and waited for him to continue.

"I'll give you half of everything."

I almost fell off the sofa. "What? What are you talking about?" I shook my head as if to clear it.

"If you stay married to me, I'll give you half of my trust fund."

"Let me get this right, you want me to condemn myself to a living hell—"

"More like purgatory."

"Okay then. So, you want me to live in purgatory indefinitely for a lousy inheritance."

"Not indefinitely. Just six months. And I'm set to inherit two billion dollars."

I opened my mouth and then closed it. I opened it again and then closed it.

"I think I feel sick. Who has that kind of money? How'd your dad make that much money? Steal it from God?" I leaned my head against the back of the couch. One billion dollars. He was going to give me one billion dollars. Now I began to feel a little ripped off that Oliver had only given me five grand for the trip. To a billionaire, five thousand dollars was probably like fifty cents to us regular people.

"So you're offering to give me a billion dollars if I stay married to you?"

"Yes, exactly—but I mean, in name only. You can still lead your life. Have your freedom. I just… well we just need to convince Dad that we're a couple."

"That shouldn't be too hard. I can be civil when I need to be."

Jude chuckled dryly. "Yes, you can be quite charming when you need to be."

I didn't like his tone, but I couldn't help the smile that tugged at the corner of my lips. "You're mocking me."

"I sure am," he sat down next to me and placed a hand over mine.

"So what do you say, Lacey? One billion dollars and all you have to do is pretend to like me."

"Hmmm... that'll be a stretch worth more than a billion dollars."

"Ouch," he joked.

I laughed and then quickly became serious. "You know, we'll need ground rules. And what if I, I don't know, want to date someone—"

"Are you serious? From what I understand you're perpetually single."

"Hey!"

"That's what Misha said."

"Misha has a big mouth."

"I think she's charming," he said with a small smile.

"She's married," I snapped.

He smiled widely then, "Jealous?"

I opened my mouth to deliver a stinging reply and decided to actually act my age. I knew he was ribbing me, trying to get a rise out of me. I felt like I'd been arguing with him since we'd first met. Somehow he brought out my passionate side, which I didn't even know I had. A lot had changed in the span of 24 hours. I'd changed, or maybe I'd always been like this and never gave myself a chance to live a little. Yes, that was it. I was repressed. Leave it to Vegas to bring out my wild, passionate and promiscuous side.

I sighed. "I'm not jealous. It's just that if we're going to fake a marriage, the least you can do is not point out how hot my friends are."

"Does that mean you're in?" He looked resplendent.

"Like I said, I'm leaning towards yes, but I have a few rules I would like to cover first."

"Of course." He nodded eagerly like an excited school boy.

"First of all, no more of this," I said, gesturing between us.

He looked confused. "Nudity? Day sex?"

I scowled. "No! No more sex in general. No more sex." I sounded shrill, but I didn't care. I had to stop having sex with the guy. It had only happened twice and one of those times I couldn't remember, but I was starting to feel like an addict and Jude was my drug. I couldn't let myself become addicted to Jude or his penis.

He frowned. "A sexless marriage sounds miserable."

"For goodness sake, Jude. It won't be a real marriage.

And we're all making sacrifices here. I'm pretending to want to be married to an oversexed man-boy—"

"And I'm pretending to want to be married to an undersexed shrew. Got it."

I wanted to be mad, but the twinkle in his eye made it clear that he was joking.

"You're so annoying. Putting up with that should be worth at least an extra million."

He stuck out his hand, "Consider it done."

"1.1 billion dollars?" I asked as I shook his hand in a no-nonsense manner.

"Yep."

"I want it in writing."

"Err... I'd rather my attorney not know."

"Then find another attorney, Jude."

"You're so bossy."

"I know."

"I like it," he said, tugging me towards him. I tried to push away, but his grip was tight.

"What are you doing?" He was still wearing only a robe and I was getting distracted by the skin I could see. Woah, girl. Calm down.

"I thought we could seal the deal with a kiss, you know like in the movies..."

"I'm not sure what type of movies you've been watching, but no thank you," I pushed away from him again and this time he let me go.

I placed my hands on my hips. "If we're going to do this, then number one is physical stuff and number two..."

"Hold on. No physical stuff at all?"

"Jude, I already said no sex."

"Okay, got that, but does that mean no blow jobs, hand jobs, heavy petting while watching movies…"

I wanted to punch him. I couldn't tell if he were being deliberately thick-headed or not. "None of the above."

"Can I at least watch you shower?"

"Jude!"

"What? I promise to be quiet."

"That's so creepy."

He smiled, "Yeah, I know. I even creeped myself out. Forget I said that. Okay, no sex or sex-like behavior. Boring. Now, what's number two?"

I frowned. What was number two? And then I remembered. "No emotions. We need to stay focused on why we're doing this and emotions would just make this arrangement messy."

He nodded. "I get it. I'll do disgusting man stuff on a daily basis so that you don't fall in love with me."

I guffawed. "You're so arrogant. If anything, you'll fall in love with me."

"You think so? Wanna bet on that?"

I was tempted. God, was I tempted, but what if I lost?

I stared at Jude, taking in the way his hair fell across his face. He was so handsome, so playful. Quick-witted and fun. He was the opposite of the men I usually dated and that was so intimidating. No, I wouldn't make a bet that I'd lose and I knew I'd surely lose this one. I was just your girl next door and he was one of the world's most eligible bachelors. This was all a charade. I was a tool to get his inheritance, or maybe he even saw me as an obstacle. It didn't matter. As much as I wanted to tell myself we were equals on the playing field, I knew we weren't. I was outmatched. Jude was in full control of the ball and I was just running around hoping that maybe he'd pass it to me once or twice.

I was glad he couldn't read my emotions as I said as nonchalantly as possible, "Maturity. Remember, Jude? We were going to be mature about this. Let's just stick to the plan and to the rules."

He seemed ready to argue, but then upon seeing the steely look in my eyes, decided against it.

"So what's the plan?" he asked me.

I didn't have a ready answer, but apparently, he had something in mind. He gestured for me to sit down. "Well, you handled the rules, let me handle the plan."

I sat down and warily said, "Do I really want to know what your plan is?"

"Hey, trust me..."

But I didn't trust him. Not even a little bit.

I placed my bags on the threshold and peeked in at the huge, unkempt, warehouse that Jude expected me to call home.

"This? This was your plan?"

I was so unimpressed. I'd been expecting at least a taste of luxury, instead, I was looking at something that resembled a warehouse after a rave. Trash was everywhere. It smelled funny and stains that I couldn't identify decorated the couch.

I was grossed out and wanted desperately to get a can of Lysol and a jug of bleach. I looked towards what I thought was the kitchen and shivered. I swore I saw something crawling.

I picked up my bags and backed up. "Nope. I can't live like this. What's one point one billion dollars worth if you can't enjoy it because you have tetanus and hepatitis?"

"My place isn't that bad," Jude said trying to bring my bags inside. I slapped at his hands.

"Jude, this place is disgusting. How do you live like this?"

"Happily."

"You need help."

"Well, I guess I could hire someone—"

"No, I mean mentally. You need help if you thought I would move into this cesspool and be okay with it."

"My feelings are so hurt."

"You don't have feelings."

"Yes, I do. Normally during football season. And soccer season. But never baseball season. Too boring. Unless feeling bored is a feeling."

I ignored him and continued to look from the safety of the door. He nudged me, or rather pushed me inside, and secured the lock on the door.

"It's not so bad once you get used to it."

"I can't get used to this, Jude. I refuse to get used to this. It's… it's… it's uninhabitable."

He looked at me as if I were nuts. He walked away from me, grabbing my bags. "I've lived here for two years. This place is great. Don't be a snob."

"I'm not a snob because I want to live in a place that doesn't have creepy crawlies in the kitchen."

He took a look at the kitchen, grimaced and said, "Yeah. I think I should call someone. I guess we should head to your place then."

"My place?!" My eyebrows shot up. Per Jude's plan, I'd live with him. He'd been rather persuasive and his plan had made sense, up until now.

"Just for a few hours until a maid makes sense of my living arrangements."

I didn't want to leave my bags in his apartment under its current conditions, so I grabbed them and stood next to the door.

"Okay. A few hours."

He took my bags from me and we made our way back to his car.

"So where do you live?"

"East downtown."

"That's not far, maybe we would have run into each other eventually."

"I doubt it. We don't run in the same circles."

"What makes you think that?"

"I'm a lowly temp worker, you're a billionaire's son and former pro-athlete."

"We have more in common than you think."

"Name one thing." I happily waited for him to answer, enjoying our banter. Even though I didn't want to admit it, he was good company. We'd actually spent a little extra time in Vegas after my friends had already flown back, to meet with a lawyer and draw up the contract. Misha and Emmaline had been surprisingly excited about our agreement. I had expected them to be judgmental and tell me I was crazy, but they hadn't. They'd seemed excited for me. Maybe it was the promise of billions of dollars that had made them open to the idea of their best friend staying married to a man she barely knew.

We'd flown home together and much to my dismay, Oliver had met us on the landing. It had been an awkward car ride. I'd wanted to talk about his health and he'd ignored all my questions and instead focused on what plans Jude and I had for our lives together. It was as if Oliver had forgotten that Jude and I had only recently met.

I didn't know what Oliver's lawyer had told him or what Jude had told his father, but Oliver was over the moon. I just wanted reassurance that I still had a job, after he assured me that I did, I tried to be receptive to his chipper mood. And for the first time since I saw them together, Oliver and Jude hadn't fought. They had almost been pleasant towards each other.

Except, as Jude and I walked to the car that waited for us Oliver had yelled to Jude, "You better not screw this up, Jude!"

"Thanks for the vote of confidence, Dad," Jude had called back.

I smiled to myself. Oliver and Jude were more alike than they realized.

"What are you smiling about?" Jude asked as we turned onto my street.

"Oh, nothing," I said.

"You know, a healthy marriage is a marriage without secrets."

"Our marriage is pretty unhealthy already given that it's based on a lie and all."

"Touché," he said as he pulled up in front of my apartment building. We climbed out and made our way upstairs.

I sensed him staring at my butt and turned around and caught him.

I shook my head as I continued up the stairs. "Seriously, Jude... you know the rules."

"What?" he gave me a sheepish, boyish grin, "I was just looking not touching. You can't blame me for enjoying the view."

I was too winded to argue with him. "Gosh, I need to get into better shape."

"Yeah, as your husband, I worry about your cardiovascular health."

I was too out of breath to be angry and just gave a resigned sigh, fished my key out of my purse and opened my door.

"Nice..." he said softly as he invited himself in. He

took his time, looking around. I immediately felt self-conscious thinking of the mansion Oliver lived in, but then I realized how silly I was being. Jude's loft had been a cesspool, speaking of which...

"Don't you have a housekeeper that you need to call?"

He shook his head. "Obviously I don't. Can you look one up for me?"

I wanted to tell him no, but realized I'd probably be a lot more efficient. I pulled out my phone and started searching for a service and was too busy focusing on the task to notice he was going through my things.

I saw him pull out my scrapbook and yelled, "Hey! Put that down!"

Of course, he ignored me. "Who's this? He looks like he's in pain."

I snatched the picture from his hand, knowing exactly what he was talking about. It was a picture of my ex-boyfriend Evan, and he did look like he was in pain. He was surrounded by a group of dogs that were ready for adoption. The picture had been taken last Christmas. I'd dragged him to a fundraiser for a local animal rescue group. He hadn't wanted to go, but I'd insisted. He'd been miserable the whole time. I swear when I wasn't looking he'd probably even kicked a puppy.

Jude sat down next to me, snatched the picture back

and studied it while scratching his chin. "He looks like a real charmer. So who is he? Ex-boyfriend?"

"Yes," I grumbled.

"Hmm... he looks like the type who would kick a puppy."

I couldn't help the giggle that escaped my mouth. "I wouldn't have put it past him. He was a jerk most days."

"So why'd you date him?"

I shrugged and quickly dialed a housekeeping service, not wanting to continue the conversation about my horrible taste in men. What was I supposed to tell Jude? That I purposefully dated losers to feel better about myself?

After I was done with my phone call Jude ambushed me with more questions.

"So what happened between you and Angry Man?"

"Evan. His name is Evan."

"Evan. That name sucks, no wonder he was so angry," he said this as he leaned his long legs out and placed his arm over the back of my chair. He took up most of the loveseat he was that big.

I tried not to think about how well-endowed he was in general as I tried to decide how much to tell him and how much not to tell him.

"Nothing really happened between us."

"He dumped you?"

I hit him with a throw pillow.

Jude grunted. "His loss."

I wasn't expecting that response and I was relieved when he seemed to be distracted by the picture frames on my faux mantle.

"Who's this?"

I got up and walked behind him. I peeked around and smiled as I took the picture from his hand.

"That's my aunt and my cousin, Leslie."

"You guys must be close."

I nodded. "She raised me."

"Oh. What happened to your parents?"

"I never knew them really."

"I'm so sorry."

My phone rang then and I happily answered. It was the housekeeping service calling me to confirm some information. I spoke to them briefly, glad for the reprieve. I didn't want to talk about my parents.

"We have to get going, the housekeeper will be there in ten minutes. Someone needs to let them in.

Two hours later Jude's loft was shiny and clean.

The guestroom was on the opposite side of the kitchen and I sat my bags in there. When I turned around I found Jude leaning up against the door with a frown on his face.

"What's wrong?"

"Come with me."

I followed him not knowing what was wrong. I

frowned at him when he stopped in front of his bedroom door.

"Is this some pitiful form of seduction?"

"No, not at all."

"My room's bigger than the guest room and since you're doing me a huge favor it only seems fair that I let you have this one."

I loved it immediately. It was front-facing with floor to ceiling windows. But I couldn't put him out of his own room.

"I love it," I confessed. "But the guest room is comfortable enough."

"Come on, take it. I want you to have it. The view is beautiful. If you're forced to live with a slob, you might as well have the best views outside of my pigsty."

"You have a point."

We both turned at the same time and bumped into each other.

I wanted to reach up and touch his chest, but I didn't. He caught my hand and looked down at it.

"You're not wearing your ring."

"I figured I'd just wear it in public."

"You should wear it now... otherwise you might forget and that would make us look very suspicious. I don't want that. Too much money is at stake."

And then to my surprise, he reached into his pocket. The ring he pulled out was stunning.

"What?"

"Surprise."

I felt stupid as my hands shook as I took the ring. It was small, yet elegant, tasteful and he slid it slowly on my finger.

I couldn't say a word. I stared at it and he reached up and tucked a loose strand of my hair behind my ear.

"Much better," he said softly.

I nodded, finding myself choked up.

"Thank you," I said. "You shouldn't have bothered."

"It's no problem, we need to make this marriage look as legitimate as possible, right? And legitimacy starts with a ring."

He had a point, but despite our deception, I couldn't help but feel warmed by his gesture. Even if it was to mislead people, the ring was sweet and thoughtful.

I looked at his wedding band and felt bad. "You're stuck with a crappy wedding band. I'll get you something else."

"I like this crappy wedding band. I'm kind of fond of it. A special lady gave it to me."

I felt myself blushing and then he bent down and kissed my cheek, I waited with baited breath for him to kiss me, but he pulled away and said, "I'll get your bags."

I shook my head... maybe this farce wasn't such a good idea after all.

8

I was sitting in Oliver's office giving him a breakdown of everything he had in his calendar for the rest of the month. I was about two minutes into my update when Oliver started coughing. It was a dry cough, but it concerned me, especially since Oliver dodged every question about his health.

"Do you want me to get you some water?"

He shook his head, "No. I'm fine. But you're boring me."

That comment caught me off guard. "What?"

"Let's talk about you instead. How's everything going with my son?"

"I… fine. I think."

"You think?" He frowned and that made me very nervous. I didn't want him concerned.

"I mean… I know everything's going fine. It's only

been a few months. So, we're definitely still newlyweds. You know, learning about each other… doing married people things." I chuckled dryly feeling highly uncomfortable. Married people things? Could I be any less eloquent? I wanted to kick myself. He hadn't asked me any direct questions about my marriage until then and I wasn't sure how to respond.

"Great. I'm glad things are going well. And since you're part of the family now, I guess you'll be going to the charity ball with Jude this year."

"The Friends of the Library Association Ball?"

"Yeah."

"Oh, I didn't know I was expected to attend."

"Jude and I attend every year. His mother sat on the board for most of her adult life. She loved public libraries. The smell of the books. The quiet. And then as she got older she helped sponsor a lot of the English language programs for resettled refugees and she raised funds for library materials in public schools."

"Those are great causes."

"Oh yes, Ophelia was a lovely woman with a huge heart. Whenever there was need, she tried to take care of it. She tried to save everyone."

"How did she pass if you don't mind me asking?"

He crossed his legs and tapped his fingers together. "I love talking about her, it's no bother. She died from complications related to Alzheimer's. At the end she barely recognized me. I could handle it, but not Jude. It really tore him up. They were very close. While Jude and I never saw eye to eye on anything, Ophelia was so accepting, so interested in all his pursuits. She was the better parent, I'm sure."

'I'm sure you tried your best."

He shook his head and his eyes grew sad. "I could have done a lot better. My best wasn't good enough for Jude. He hates me."

"That's not true." Although, I wasn't sure if I was right or not.

"I try not to dwell on it. The past is the past. I can't fix that. I'm just focusing on the future now. Speaking of which, have you two decided on how many kids you'll have?"

I wanted to run screaming from the room, but I gathered my wits about me and said, "We haven't discussed children yet."

"I hope you'll have at least two. I regret that Jude is an only child. I wish he had someone else to help him make the tough choices especially now given my condition."

I waited for him to continue, but when he didn't I knew that was the end of the conversation. He promptly changed the subject like I knew he would. He'd avoided talking about his health and Jude knew even less than I did.

When we were done I prepared to leave, about to call a taxi when Oliver stopped me.

"What are you doing? Are you still taking taxis? I thought Jude would have gotten you a car. You're family now, just take one of my cars."

"I can't do that."

"I insist."

"Oliver, you're way too generous."

"Again, you're my family now. And no family member of mine is going to have to rely on a taxi driver to get her to and from home. Now come with me and tell me which car you want."

I followed him to the garage and realized that he had three different cars lined up. One was an SUV and two were classic European cars. I didn't feel comfortable driving any of them down the street. They were too pretentious for my taste. I said this to Oliver who waved away my concerns.

"Take the SUV. You'll fit right in. Americans love SUVs... such a weird fascination," he said, almost to himself.

I figured it was better than the fancy European antiques so I grabbed the keys and jumped in. It was an Escalade and I giggled as I backed out.

"This car is really popular with rappers!" Oliver happily informed me.

I laughed and drove to Jude's. He was leaning against

his practical sedan waiting for me. When I pulled up he laughed.

"Dad gave you a car I see."

"I didn't ask him for it," I said, feeling guilty.

"Whatever. I just feel bad that I didn't think of it first."

I climbed out of the SUV and into Jude's car. Jude held the door open for me and I thought not for the first time how respectful he was. And considerate. It was hard to rationalize the man I knew now with the man I'd met what felt like ages ago.

"So what's the surprise... where are we going?"

"You'll see."

I sat back enjoying the ride. He surprised me by singing along to a few songs that I associated with teenage girls.

"Come on, sing along. You know you want to."

I shook my head. "You're doing great. I wouldn't want to interrupt the master."

He started singing falsetto and I giggled. His happiness was contagious and I found myself singing along despite my original protests. It reminded me of days long gone when I would sing with my aunt and cousin on our road trips to northern Florida to camp.

I was still singing loudly and off-key when I noticed that he was no longer singing. It was just me. We were sitting at a stoplight and he was staring at me.

"You're pretty cute when you're not uptight and cranky."

"So you think I'm cute?"

"Maybe… just a little. You're mostly just cranky."

"Oh, Jude. You're too kind."

He reached out and surprised me by stroking the side of my face. "Thanks for doing this, Lacey. I know this hasn't been easy—"

"Well you are going to pay me."

"Even so, you're sacrificing a lot to make this work and I just want you to know I appreciate it. I appreciate you. I don't take what you're doing for me for granted."

I realized then that his hand was still on my face and I found myself leaning towards him. He leaned in towards me and a loud honk sounded from behind us.

"Green light," I said softly, my lips almost touching his. He smiled regretfully and pulled off.

I stared out my window to avoid his eyes. We had one too many close calls for my comfort. Just the other night we'd fallen asleep on the couch together and I'd woken up cuddled in his arms. I'd forced myself to sneak away and go to my own room when instead I'd wanted to stay in his arms. I was concerned. This marriage was supposed to be a fake, yet it was the realest relationship I'd ever been in.

"You ready?"

I'd been so deep in thought that I hadn't noticed we'd

reached our destination. I looked around and frowned. We were in front of a dark gray building in a questionable part of town.

"Care to tell me where we are now?"

"Come on and I'll show you."

We walked in and I felt a little weirded out. The building was eerily quiet.

"Um... you aren't planning to kill me. Are you?"

"I don't think so. Should I be?"

"Haha. Not funny."

He pushed through a pair of double doors and then I saw a sign that said Ophelia's Angels. Before I could ask about it, I noticed what was going on in front of me.

The building was packed from front to back with boxes, boxes I quickly realized were full of food.

Workers were sorting food. Packers were packaging boxes. Others were shouting orders. It was a busy, well-oiled machine.

"What's Ophelia's Angels? Some sort of packaging firm?"

"Something like that. We collect donations from around the city, clothes, food, etcetera, and ship them out to seniors in the community."

"We?"

"Yes, Ophelia's Angels is—"

"Named after your mother. This is your organization?"

Jude nodded. "Yeah, I started it when she first started getting sick."

"Did she know about it?"

He shook his head. "She passed away so quickly, we were still getting off the ground when she died."

I found myself taking his hand. "I'm sure she would have been proud of you."

He nodded. "So now you know my secret, tell me about your family."

I dropped his hand and moved away. "You already know I was raised by my aunt."

"What happened to your parents?"

I sighed, knowing that I couldn't continue dodging his questions. "I never knew my mother. I was raised by my father, but I don't remember him either because he died when I wasn't even one."

"I'm so sorry."

"It's okay. I had a great childhood. My aunt treated me like a daughter and my cousin Leslie was a blast. My aunt was very loving. It's just that I grew up on the wrong side of the tracks per se. I was bused into the richer neighborhoods for school and the kids there never let me forget that I was the poor kid, only there because of a scholarship. They made it clear that I didn't fit in there."

"Rich kids are the worst. You weren't missing much."

I guffawed. "Says a rich kid."

He held up his hands. "Actually, my dad disowned me years ago."

"What? You're kidding."

He shook his head. "I wish I were. But he cut me off when I was twenty."

"So how are you funding this operation?"

"Mom left me some property and I saved some money from when I played pro-ball, but I wanted to expand outside of the city to other states, even internationally eventually. Right now, I don't have the funds to make that happen, but one day..."

I nodded in understanding. "That's why your inheritance is such a big deal to you."

He nodded. "I'm not some spoiled rich boy. I mean, I was. But life has a way of throwing things at you, pulling the rug from under you that makes you stop and pay attention."

"Don't I know it! I woke up naked next to a stranger in Vegas who I thought was a billionaire but turns out is a broke CEO of a nonprofit."

"Disappointed?"

"Not even a little. You're an enigma, Mr. Foster."

"I'll take that as a compliment given other things I'm sure you've called me behind my back."

"You misjudge me. I only talk badly about you when you're within earshot. What's the fun of trash talking you when you can't hear me?"

I smiled broadly as he laughed. "You're a woman of integrity, Lacey."

He took my hand, surprising me.

"What are you doing?"

"I want to introduce you to my crew, you know since you're my wife and all."

I felt honored for some reason, but I told myself not to give into the feeling. Our marriage was a farce; he was only doing his due diligence.

I was lost in thought and was surprised when he pulled me into a conference room where a meeting was underway. There were about six people sitting around a long oval conference table engaged in animated conversation that abruptly stopped when they noticed me.

I saw a few grins and appraising looks and was suddenly self-conscious. I reached up to make sure my hair wasn't a complete mess and smiled brightly at the group in front of me.

"Everyone, this is Lacey, my wife."

"So the rumors are true? I thought you'd dreamed it all," said a young dark-skinned man with a light Caribbean accent. He wore glasses and a dress shirt with a tie. He was dressed more for a corporate environment instead of a casual day at the office like the others who wore jeans and plain t-shirts.

"Lacey, meet Aidan. He's my VP. And apparently he thinks I'm delusional and made you up."

Aidan smiled wide and said with a shrug, "It wouldn't be the first time. It's a pleasure to meet you."

I wasn't sure if I should have offered my hand or just nod, so I returned his smile and waved my fingers at him. *God, I was awkward.*

I then nervously did the same with the others who went around introducing themselves and explaining who they were in the operation. And then Jude surprised me by saying, "Alright Lacey, so I'll let you get acquainted. Aidan, can you join me in my office?"

And as soon as they disappeared the others sat there in silence staring at me.

"Sooo…." said one of them whose name I couldn't remember. "You're Jude's wife…"

I nodded and nervously looked down at my ring. "Yep. I guess I am." I felt so stupid. I guess? Gosh, what was wrong with me? I was about to cast doubt in everyone's mind that our marriage was real.

"I mean, yep. I'm Mrs. Jude Foster," I laughed nervously and sank into a chair. "Soooo…." I said changing the subject "What's Jude like as a boss? Tell me all the dirt."

"He's cheap. He hasn't bought us lunch in weeks."

The rest of them began to laugh and I realized it was a joke. I awkwardly laughed with them.

"But seriously, Jude's a great boss. This is by far the

best team I've been on and hey, he's really nice to look at, not that you haven't noticed."

I laughed, finally loosening up. "I guess he's okay looking," I said with a casual shrug.

We sat around joking and getting better acquainted. Jude peeked his head around the corner.

"Want to help out with the operation today?"

I nodded enthusiastically. The next thing I knew, I was packing boxes with Jerry and helping Anna with a few social media tasks.

Before I knew it, five o'clock had rolled around and I was exhausted.

"You can tell you guys are newlyweds," Anna said with a laugh.

"Oh really? How's that?"

"He doesn't stop looking at you. I caught him a few times staring at you and he always looks the other way and pretends to be doing something else. It's really cute."

I blushed, unsure what to say. I'd thought it was my imagination, but I could feel his eyes on me most of the day. And a few times when I thought he wasn't looking, I'd found myself staring at him. I felt like I'd seen a whole new side to him. I saw how much he cared about the cause and the people he helped. I admired him. He hadn't just withdrawn when his mother was dying, he'd done something to help others. I found myself proud of him and feeling so much respect for the man he was.

I waited for him in his office while he said goodbye to his staff.

He came back in and exhaustedly collapsed into his chair.

I leaned my elbow against the desk and put my chin in my hand. "Tired?"

"I'm beat," he said rubbing his forehead.

"Got a headache?"

He shook his head. "I think I have the beginnings of one, though. It was just a busier day than usual for a slow day—"

My eyebrows shot up. "A slow day? This is the busiest company I've ever worked at."

"So did you enjoy your time here?"

"It was great. Anna, Jerry, even no-nonsense Aidan is growing on me."

"They're a great group and they seemed to really like you."

"You're being nice."

"I'm not. I enjoy being around you, most people do."

I narrowed my eyes and said playfully, "You just want me around for free labor." I was admittedly trying to lighten the mood with humor. I hadn't expected the compliment. It had made feel special. *No emotions, Lacey. Remember your rules.*

"I want you around for a lot more than that," he said quietly and his tone wasn't playful anymore.

"Well there are like a billion dollars at stake, so yeah there's that too."

He ignored my comment and said softly, "Come here, Lacey."

"No, I think I'll stay on this side of the desk."

"Okay then." He stood up and came over to me.

He stood in front of me and crooked his finger. I shook my head. I felt if I stayed seated I could control myself.

Apparently, Jude had other plans.

In one smooth motion, he picked me up and placed me on the edge of the desk. He started kissing my neck and I moaned when his lips finally met mine. He slid his hands between my legs, raising my dress up so that the skirt was around my hips. He parted my thighs, spreading them wide, and stood between them, alternating between rubbing my heated sex and kissing my face, my eyes, my cheeks.

He pushed me back onto the desk and freed my breasts from the constraints of my dress and bra.

His warm mouth pulled at my nipples and I grabbed his face, trying to keep him there.

"Oh god, Jude," I groaned as he roughly sucked my nipple, alternating between one breast and the other.

I felt his hand between my legs and gasped as he moved my panties to the side and dipped a finger into me, stroking me, making me crave him like I'd never craved him before.

I shimmied a little to get my skirt further up and parted my legs wantonly, turned on by the thought of forbidden office sex, coupled with the eagerness that Jude displayed, as if he couldn't wait to be inside me.

He reached into his pocket, put on a condom, and rid me of my panties, sliding into my wetness in one pleasurable stroke. I brought my hips up to meet his thrusts, burying the heels of my feet into his bare buttocks with every thrust.

Comically, the desk below me rocked loudly each time he pushed into me. But I didn't care. I could feel my insides squeezing around him and I knew I was about to come, but I wanted to enjoy it a little bit more. I wanted to enjoy the feel of Jude buried inside me just a little longer.

"Don't stop, Jude, please don't stop," I managed to moan.

"I wouldn't dream of it," he said, before kissing me again and pushing me over the edge as he slowly pulled out of me and then with incredible slowness, pushed himself deep into my waiting wetness, inch by inch.

The pleasure was so intense that I held my breath. I couldn't breathe. Couldn't think. And then I started to come. My body shook all over as he buried his head in the crook of my neck.

"Oh God, Lacey. You feel so good," he said, and I could feel him coming too. My sex squeezed his, determined to memorize the feel of him.

He thrust into me one last time and my hips drove upwards as I came again.

"Jude!" I shouted as my head hurt from the force of my orgasm.

And then we were spent, holding each other. He slowly pulled out of me and I made an involuntary groan, saddened as I missed his warmth.

He extended his hand and pulled me up from the desk. He pulled up his pants and helped me arrange my clothes.

I was afraid to look in his eyes, but I knew I had to say something. We were quickly crossing the point of no return and one of us had to do something about it.

I opened my mouth to speak when he stopped everything I had to say by kissing me thoroughly on the mouth.

He then pulled back slowly and placed a finger against my lips, quieting my next words.

"Let's go home," he said, taking my hand in his and ushering me through the door.

9

I stood in front of the mirror staring at myself. I couldn't take my eyes off my reflection. I was dressed in a long evening gown that was most likely the most elegant item of clothing I'd ever owned (not to mention, the most expensive). It was black, off-the-shoulder and fit like a glove. I'd never worn anything so close fitting so naturally, I was uncomfortable.

"Would you stop pulling at it?" Emmaline said for the second time in the past five minutes.

I gave her an annoyed look before saying, "Stop being so bossy."

She laughed. "I'm just saying that you look great. Stop fussing with your dress."

I couldn't help but not take her advice as I attempted to hike the top part of the dress further up. I felt the dress didn't do enough to keep my important parts hidden, but what did I know? Emmaline was right. I looked pretty darn good.

"Do you think this bust line is way too low?"

"Nope. Your boobs are supposed to look like they're about to spill out."

I frowned, "Really? That's a good look?"

"Trust me. I might not be very fashionable, but I know fashion."

"Yeah, that doesn't make any sense," I said, mostly to myself because Emmaline was looking down at her phone.

"Hey, a little attention here."

"Sorry," she said, burying her phone under a pillow.

"Were you texting someone?" I narrowed my eyes at her.

"What? No! That was no one."

I could hear her phone beeping incessantly under her pillow.

"Go ahead and get it."

She bit her lip as if deciding whether to keep playing coy, decided against it and dove for her phone. I watched her smile spread from ear to ear as she read the text messages. Whatever was being said, she was apparently happy to hear it.

Her daughter, Theodora, came running in and gushed at the sight of me.

"Auntie Lacey you look sooooooooo beautiful."

"Thank you so much," I beamed. I'd let my hair grow out over the months and it was now hanging down around my shoulders. I had to get used to the longer length which seemed to frame my face perfectly. Emmaline had let me borrow her shoes and had helped me with my makeup. The result was stunning. The sexy dark red color made my lips look pouty and inviting. And my eye makeup gave me a hint of mystery. I was like a new woman. Glamorous, mysterious, and oh so nervous about tonight.

"You're going to be the most beautiful woman at the ball."

I laughed. "You think so, Dora?"

"I know so. Jude is going to freak when he sees you."

I secretly hoped she was right. I wanted Jude's attention more than anything tonight. It had been three weeks since the incident in his office and we'd continued our lives as if nothing had happened.

We didn't talk about it. We didn't repeat it. And to my disappointment, Jude had kept his distance. He worked late and came home even later. I rarely saw him anymore. He wasn't cold towards me, just distant. Gone was the flirtatious banter and furtive, meaningful looks when he thought I wouldn't notice. We never again snuggled on the couch or went anywhere together. We were living two different lives under one roof and although it had been both our ideas to make the charade work, I couldn't help but feel a little resentful that it all was a charade. I would never admit it out loud, but I wanted more from Jude.

I'd decided to go to Emmaline's to get dressed because I had no idea what to wear and I needed help with my makeup for the evening. Misha was busy at a convention, but she'd wished me good luck. She adored Jude and I think she knew how I really felt about him. Which was funny, because I wasn't even sure how I felt about Jude.

Speaking of which, I'd given Jude Emmaline's address and I had to admit, I was nervous as I waited for him to arrive. I wondered how he'd react. I stared at myself in the mirror, feeling different. I didn't think I'd ever find myself in this predicament. I didn't feel like myself and emotionally I didn't know what I wanted. I was the decisive type, but my feelings for Jude made me second-guess myself, which made me feel vulnerable. I hated feeling like that.

A knock sounded at the door and I listened intently. It didn't take long for me to hear the sound of his voice and I instantly smiled at it.

I made my way towards him, nervously tugging at the bust line of my dress. He was turned away from me, so he couldn't hear me as I approached.

He was in a serious conversation with Theodora

about something. She was animated as she spoke to him and laughed at something he said before spotting me. She smiled in my direction and Jude turned towards me.

"You look beautiful," were his first words to me as he stood slowly and I finally got a good look at him. He was wearing a tuxedo that made him look powerful and untouchable. I gulped hard. This man was so out of my league. What was I thinking?

But apparently, he thought otherwise as he quickly moved towards me and took me by my hand. His brown eyes examined me from head to toe. And he twirled me in a circle, making me giggle. He made me feel young, beautiful, and carefree. I loved that feeling when I was around him. It was like I had the old Jude back tonight. I smiled in relief.

He let out a low whistle and I heard Theodora giggle.

I blushed, saying, "Well, I think we should head on out."

"See you later, Lacey," Theodora called out.

"Have fun, Lacey!" Emmaline called and then she winked at me and made a face that made me blush.

I was surprised to see the limousine waiting for us out front. He took my hand in the limo and said once again how beautiful I looked. I expected him to kiss me, but to my surprise, he didn't even try.

I felt dejected, but told myself to not think too much

of it. To my surprise, he held my hand the entire time, staring out the window and not saying anything.

The silence became maddening and I felt the need to say something, anything. "Are you not going to talk to me the entire night?"

He looked at me sharply, as if taken aback by my blunt words. He smiled at me, but his eyes were guarded. He touched my face gently.

"I'm sorry. I just have a lot on my mind. This ball always makes me a little nostalgic."

I instantly felt bad for making this night all about me. Of course he was sad. This whole evening probably reminded him of his mother.

"I'm sorry."

"It's okay, I just wish—" he laughed humorlessly. "Never mind."

"No," I urged him. "Tell me. What is it that you wish?"

"Another time," he said as the car pulled up. "We're here."

He got out first and extended me his hand. As he helped me out of the car, cameras flashed in all directions and I wasn't prepared for them. I instantly attempted to hide my face, grabbing Jude's hand and practically forcing him along.

He laughed and said, "How do you walk so quickly in those heels?"

"Years of being a girl come in handy."

We climbed the stairs that led to the stately library and entered a small room that bore Ophelia's name.

The room was lined with books and I realized the room led to an even bigger hall. Oliver warmly greeted us, but then he was swept away by a group of distinguished-looking men around his age.

When he was gone, Jude looked around and said softly, "This was my mother's favorite room. She spent so much time here that I had them dedicate it to her after she passed." He gestured towards a small table. "I would sit across from her scribbling my letters. Drawing pictures."

I could easily imagine him as a little boy. And his mind seemed to be recalling the image as well as he stared at the desk, before reluctantly looking away. "Enough about me. Let me introduce you to some of mom's friends."

We spent the rest of the night hearing stories about his mom from nearly everyone who greeted us. She was much loved and missed, that was certainly clear. Despite everyone being very welcoming and nice, I was feeling overwhelmed. The photographers, the people, the opulence of it all, mixed with my unclear feelings toward Jude, was starting to wear on me and I could feel tension forming in my shoulders.

I excused myself and found my way to a balcony. I

was enjoying the air, wondering what to do next. *How could I start a conversation with Jude about how I felt?* I needn't have worried because I was so occupied with my own thoughts that I didn't hear him when he joined me on the balcony.

He placed a hand on my lower back and said softly, "Mind if I join you?"

"I wish you could have met her. She would have liked you." He said without waiting for me to answer his earlier question.

I smiled. "Do you like me?"

"I more than like you, Mrs. Foster, but I'm sure you already know that."

"You're just saying that."

He kissed me then, catching me off-guard. I pressed against him, unable to get enough. I needed him. The feel of him. The smell of him. My body yearned for him as much as my heart. I had fallen in love with Jude. Love. That was what I felt.

And before I could second-guess myself, I spoke the words, "I love you, Jude."

He didn't sound surprised nor did he hesitate, responding simply with, "Not as much as I love you."

My heart was pounding and I couldn't even take a breath and then I heard Oliver call his name before he peeked out and found us.

"Hi, lovebirds, sorry to interrupt, but I need to borrow you for a little bit."

Jude kissed my cheek and disappeared with his father.

I watched him go, feeling elated. I wanted to sing, jump in the air and cheer. I was in love. He loved me back.

I meandered over to the other side of the balcony, looking out over the gardens when I heard voices near me. There were a group of ladies standing with their backs towards me, talking rather loudly. I assumed they had too much to drink and with amusement, I did a little eavesdropping.

"So what do you think? Is she just after his money?"

Oh, this is juicy, I thought to myself leaning in a bit to catch the other person's response.

"Clearly," said the other woman.

"Definitely a rags to riches story. I heard she's originally from the South, broke, no parents, raised by her aunt. She's lucky she hit the jackpot."

My shoulders tensed. They were talking about me.

"More like she won the lottery. She must have been so excited. From trailer park to a mansion. Lucky girl."

"I don't know," one of the ladies laughed cruelly. "Can you really picture Jude falling for a woman like her? I mean, consider the girls he's dated in the past. He's never had any interest in white trash before. If anything, out of desperation, Oliver probably planned the whole thing and threatened Jude with losing his inheritance if he didn't comply. You know how much he wanted to control Jude's life."

"I heard Oliver isn't even dying," said another, and the others nodded in agreement. "He has both those young folks doing his bidding and it's all based on a lie."

At least she didn't call me trailer trash, she just felt sorry for me, I thought to myself, but I didn't know what stung more.

"We all know it's not a real marriage," said the cruel one again. "He's the city's most eligible bachelor and he marries her? It was a matter of convenience arranged by Oliver who knew that girl wouldn't walk away from millions. And he knew that Jude wouldn't let her. He's just a broke, ex-athlete. He needs his daddy's money."

The old ladies nodded in agreement and I backed away, not knowing I was crying until I felt the tears slipping down my cheeks.

So that's what they thought of me? They thought I was trailer trash. They thought that I was able to be bought. And then my anger dissipated. Isn't that exactly what happened? Didn't I agree to this farce of a relationship for money? They were right. I was just as much at fault as Oliver. And maybe he had planned all of this, but I'd been a willing accomplice.

I knew what I had to do. I made my way outside, walking past the confused faces of Oliver and Jude.

Jude caught up with me easily.

"Hey, where are you going so fast?"

"Out of here."

"So soon? And without me? I'm pretty sure we came together."

I said nothing. I couldn't speak right then. I was too upset.

He grabbed my arm, stopping me. "What's wrong, Lacey?"

I began to cry. "All of this. This whole scam of a marriage. Us. We're what's wrong. I don't know who's conning who."

"What's that supposed to mean?"

"Just how convenient was it that your dad would send me to Vegas and you would come along? How convenient that he was dying."

"You're trying to say my dad planned all of this? That he's faking his own impending doom?" He scoffed, "Tell me you don't actually believe that, Lacey."

"I don't know what I believe," I said. "I just know I can't continue with this farce anymore."

"Farce? What I feel for you isn't a farce."

"Really, Jude? Is that what you really believe? Because you weren't even interested in me before all this—before this stupid ruse."

"That's not true—"

"Don't lie. Seriously, don't do this." He grabbed my arm stopping me from moving. "Listen to me, Lacey."

"No! I'm tired of this charade. I want out, ok."

"But Lacey, I need you—"

"I'm sorry about leaving Ophelia's Angels in a bind, but I'm sure you'll find a way to raise enough money to keep it going."

"This isn't about that—"

I was done listening. "I can't do this."

I stuck my hand out and flagged a taxi.

One stopped for me immediately and I climbed in.

I didn't make eye contact with Jude and as I slid into the taxi; I knew I was never going to see him again. Despite myself, I couldn't stop from looking behind me. I saw him standing there just staring after me.

I hated the way I felt at that moment. With a heavy heart, I began to sob.

"Emmaline, I'm so sorry," I whispered hastily as I stood at the threshold of her front door, waiting for her to let me in.

She blinked at me repeatedly in surprise and rubbed at her eyes. "What? What are you doing here? Come in."

"I'm so sorry, I hope I didn't wake Theodora."

I didn't complete my thought as a voice interrupted me. "Everything okay, Emmie?"

I recognized that voice and my mouth opened to a perfect O as I saw who was standing there behind Emmaline, shirtless with messy hair.

"Hi, Lacey. Long time no see."

I smiled and wiped my nose on my sleeve. I was snotty from way too much crying and had taken a taxi straight from the event to Emmaline's home because I didn't want to go back to Jude's loft. I had foolishly given up the lease on my apartment figuring that I could look for another one after the six months with Jude were up.

Stupid, stupid, stupid, I thought to myself.

"Hi, Colin."

We awkwardly hugged. I hadn't seen him since college and it was a shocker frankly to see him again, half-dressed in Emmaline's home.

"Umm… so when did you two get back together? When did this happen?"

Colin and Emmaline looked at each other.

She placed a hand against his chest and said, "Give us a little privacy, ok?"

He kissed her solidly on the mouth. "Don't take too long."

He then walked away from me. "It's good to see you again, Lacey."

I smiled, still confused by his presence. As soon as he disappeared through the door, I said, "What are you doing? What's Colin doing here? When did this all start?"

"I thought you were here to talk about you?"

I narrowed my eyes at her and sat down hard on the couch. "Spill it."

"It's been going on for at least a year."

"A year!" I hadn't been expecting that!

"Yeah. It just sort of happened," she said, smiling.

"I've spent years pushing him away, determined to not need him, but I've needed him all this time. I was being stupid. And I ended up hurting both Theodora and myself in the process. What's the saying? Pride cometh before the fall? I was so determined that I could be a great single mom despite my age, that I refused the love and help of my child's father. I was so stupid… we even considered getting married in Vegas when we met up—"

"Hold on. Rewind. You two met up in Vegas? When we were all together? Like on our trip?"

She blushed. "Yeah. Sorry about that. He just popped up. I wasn't expecting that. I actually went to Vegas to get over him. We had just had an argument and I was determined to end it with him, but he showed up at the bar that night—"

"So, that's why you weren't around to save me from myself!? I got beat up, you know. Jude had to rescue me."

She nodded. "Yeah. Sorry about that. I was too busy making out with my ex in the hallway…. where unfortunately, Misha caught us."

"So Misha knows too? I feel so left out of the loop!" I narrowed my eyes at her. "So is that why you were MIA the next day when I found out that I had married Jude?"

She nodded guiltily. "I was hiding Colin in my bedroom."

I shook my head. "So did you guys get hitched too?"

"Oh no! Even in our inebriated state, we realized that

would cause a lot of confusion for Theodora, so we wanted to do it the right way."

I frowned. "Why couldn't I have had your sense of practicality when drunk?"

She laughed. "Yeah, I did sigh in relief and thank God I hadn't done what you did."

"Thanks, Emmaline. Thanks for that," I said sarcastically and then softened my tone. "Honestly, I'm so happy for you. I always thought you and Colin were good together. And I'm sure Theodora will love having her parents back together."

She nodded. "We plan to tell her soon. As in tomorrow morning when she wakes up."

I frowned. "I hope I didn't wake her by knocking, and she's sitting somewhere eavesdropping."

Emmaline waved off my concerns. "That girl could sleep through a natural disaster. You're fine. Let's get back to you. What are you going to do about Jude?"

"Walk away. No, run away. With the last of my dignity."

"Okayyyyy," she said drawing the word out and giving me a long look. "Let's try again. What's going on? Why are you here? You were so excited about tonight and about you and Jude."

I quickly told Emmaline what I had heard and she listened, interrupting only to ask a question to clarify some of the things I said.

And when I was done, I expected her to tear into them. I expected her to say that I was right to have left, that those people were horrible and that I shouldn't even waste my breath on them.

Instead, she said, "Those people aren't Oliver. They aren't Jude. I think you overreacted, Lacey."

"What the hell? Seriously, Emmaline. Someone calls me white trash and you think I should have just stuck around and thanked them." I was beyond hurt. How could Emmaline not take my side? Didn't she remember how we'd been treated as kids? "It's like you've forgotten about our childhood. It's like you don't remember how we were treated by those spoiled ass rich kids. Damn, Emmaline, have you forgotten that we've come from nothing?" I stood up, trying to hold back the tears that were threatening to fall.

Emmaline chuckled dryly. "Nope, I remember. I remember every humiliating moment of high school. I remember how the rich kids taunted us, made fun of us, made us feel as if we didn't belong there."

"Yet you think I overreacted?" I said, the tears now flowing freely as I thought of all the horrible things the kids had said and done.

"I think you're misplacing your anger. Jude didn't say those things. Jude has never treated you as anything other than an equal. And Oliver, it seems he liked you the moment he met you. You have a chip on your shoulder, Lacey."

"You don't know what you're talking about—"

Emmaline's eyebrows arched and I knew she was mad. "I don't know what I'm talking about? I'm a woman who was born into poverty and got knocked up in college. I'm the one who insisted on being a single mother and doing it all on my own because I refused to accept the love and help of the one man who unconditionally and wholeheartedly wanted to give me both." Her voice shook. "I had a huge chip on my shoulder, Lacey. And what do I have to show for it? I denied my daughter the gift of living with both her parents under one roof because I wanted to prove to others that Emmaline Daniels might have been poor and from the wrong side of the tracks, but she could do it all on her own. And what do I have to show for it?"

She waited for me to answer, but I didn't know what to say. I didn't know she had ever felt that way.

"I'll tell you what I have to show for it… I missed out on ten years of being with the man I loved and raising my child with the father she loved, all because of some misplaced pride and you shouldn't do the same. We're not those poor kids anymore. We're not just trash from the wrong side of the track. We're adults with choices and we need to start making better ones."

I sat down defeated. I knew she was right.

"You know," I said in a small voice. "Their words hurt so much because I couldn't help thinking, what if they're right? Am I really good enough for Jude? And God, I did agree to this arrangement for the money. So what does that say about me? It says I'm desperate."

"Honey, there are women who marry incarcerated serial killers just to become famous. Compared to them, I think you're doing okay. If there's a scale of desperate women, I'm sure you're not on it."

I giggled. My giggle turned into laughter and we were laughing so hard we didn't know Theodora was there until she stood in front of us looking sleepy and agitated.

"Can you two hold it down? Some of us are trying to sleep, you know. I do have responsibilities, specifically a school project tomorrow."

"Oops, sorry," I said sheepishly.

"Sorry," Emmaline echoed. With a sigh of frustration, Theodora walked back to her room.

Emmaline smothered a giggle. "What did I tell you? She's ten going on eighteen."

I chuckled and placed my hand over hers. "Thanks for hearing me out. Helping me see reason."

"That's what friends are for. I just don't want you to throw away a good thing. And what you have with Jude is a very good thing."

"He said he loved me tonight…"

"Of course he does. How could he not?"

I hugged her and stood up to leave when I realized my only choice was a hotel or back to the loft.

"Do you mind if I spend the night here?"

"No, I don't mind, but I think it would better if you go home and face your demons."

"You mean, face Jude"

"Yep."

"Call me a cab?"

"I'll just drop you off."

We pulled up in front of the loft and I looked at her. "Wish me luck,"

I hopped out the car as Emmaline made a U-turn and yelled out, "Go get him, girl!"

I squared my shoulders as if I were going into battle and made my way to the door. I took a deep breath and inserted my key.

Before I could turn the lock, the door was opening from the other side. Looking tired and pissed off, Jude stood there.

I opened my mouth to say something, anything, but nothing came out.

He said nothing to me, just studied me, his eyes not revealing any emotions. He turned away from me and I avoided the inevitable as long as possible, taking my time to lock and bolt the door.

He went to the fridge, pulled out a beer and sat down

on the couch and used the end table to open his beer, smacking the cap with his hand, sending the cap spiraling across the floor. I stared at the cap since it seemed the better option instead of facing Jude. Apparently, he had other ideas.

"I'm over here, Lacey. At the very least, you can look at me."

I forced myself to.

"Why'd you run from me tonight?"

I shrugged and looked away from him, not because I didn't know the answer, but because I didn't even know where to start. So I just started talking and hoped he would understand.

"When we met, I didn't even have my own car, Jude—"

He made a face, clearly confused. "What does that have to do with us?"

"You're a son of a billionaire, a former athlete who's been around the world. You have connections to all sorts of people. I was just a lowly temp worker. A nobody. Our meeting and marrying was like a Cinderella story, but instead of it being based on love, it was based on greed and deception."

"A Cinderella story?" he said incredulously.

"Yeah, the handsome prince rescuing the lowly servant girl."

"Rescue you? I didn't rescue you, Lacey. Our story

isn't some sort of Cinderella tale. We were both consenting adults who helped each other. In fact, I needed you a lot more than you needed me. You were doing fine without me. Better than fine."

"Oh please, I didn't have a steady job, a car, a—"

"Stop. Stop downing yourself and your life. You know why my dad chose you as his assistant?"

I shrugged.

"He liked you. He knew upon meeting you that you had integrity, a backbone, you were a fighter and he liked that. You weren't intimidated by either of us. You were like a schoolmaster… except much more attractive."

I shook my head. "You're just being nice."

"No, I'm being truthful. Most people, when dealt a heavy hand in life, just fold. But not you, Lacey. You step up to challenges. Working for my father is a challenge, being my wife is a challenge and you've accepted those challenges head on. Yeah, it's not a Cinderella story because you don't need a knight or a prince to rescue you, you rescued yourself. And if you can't see that, then you seriously can't see yourself the way others see you. The way I see you. I see a courageous woman, someone who's not afraid to take risks or chances. I see a woman who took a chance on me."

"I stayed with you for money, Jude. Stop making me out to be this great person."

"No, I convinced you to stay with me for money. Because I would have used whatever ploy I could to get you to stay with me. Why do you think I never took my ring off, Lacey? I didn't regret marrying you for a second. Not one second."

I shook my head, feeling tears flood my eyes. This couldn't be true.

"Remember, I was cut off. I would have found a way to expand Ophelia's Angels without my Dad's help. No, this agreement was about me getting you to stay with me. It was about us. I wanted to see if we could make us work."

"So you did set this all up? You and your father?"

"Unless he gave us both roofies, I'm not sure how that could be so. At the end of the day, we married each other because we wanted to."

"And we stayed together because of money…"

"You honestly believe that?"

I didn't answer him and he stood up, crossed the space between us and sat down next to me, folding his hands around mine.

"What can I do to make this right? How can I get you to understand that I love you? That you're special to me. Vegas only accelerated the inevitable. I love you, Lacey. A billion dollars doesn't change that."

He was stroking my face, breaking down my resolve,

but in the back of my mind, I could hear the voices of those women.

"They'll never accept me in your circle. They think I'm a gold digger." I told him what I heard and his eyes darkened. He was angry.

"Every single one of those women married into money. And half of them are now widows who every now and then throw themselves at my dad. In fact, some of them didn't even wait until my mother was dead to try to tempt my father."

"That's disgusting."

"They're disgusting. Jealous. Petty. So whatever they said about you is just a reflection of themselves. It's probably the same things they said about my mother."

"Your mother wasn't from a wealthy family?" I was surprised.

Jude laughed, hard. "Mom was the youngest of five kids. She was raised by a cousin. She never knew her parents. They were so broke they had dirt floors growing up. She was from West Virginia. A beautiful place, but as soon as she was old enough, she left, came to the big city. She met my dad at a gas station where she worked as a cashier."

"You're kidding me."

"Nope."

"Every day he went to see her and they'd chat. After six months she finally agreed to go out with him."

"Oh… and then they fell in love?"

"Well, Dad fell in love at first sight, it took Mom another two years to convince."

I laughed. "I'm sorry I left. I just felt so out of my element in your world."

"My world?" he said softly, cupping my face. He shook his head. "No, you don't understand. *You* are my world."

I swallowed hard. I knew he meant every word. Every part of my being, my heart, my soul, my spirit, yearned to be a part of Jude's world. And then it dawned on me: as much as I was his world, for the rest of my life, he would be mine.

EXTENDED EPILOGUE - BILLIONAIRE IN VEGAS

"*E*veryone, say cheese!"

"Cheese!" we responded, smiling brightly at the camera.

"God this is such a lovely wedding!" Misha gushed.

I looked around me. People I hadn't seen in years were gathered there.

My aunt and cousin Leslie were somewhere among them. It was a truly a special day. Emmaline's and Colin's special day.

"Emmaline made such a beautiful bride," I said.

It had been a small wedding, but emotional and heartfelt. I think I even saw Theodora trying to hide her tears as her parents spoke their vows to each other.

And to my surprise, I'd even seen Emmaline's parents. Emmaline had been equally surprised to see them, and I assumed Colin had invited them given how

Emmaline walked away from them as soon as they'd appeared at the rehearsal dinner. I knew they hadn't spoken in at least a decade. I'd moved to go talk to her when I saw Collin following behind her. I stayed out of it. It was a family matter. Emmaline had eventually come out, but had ignored her parents.

But things seemed to be on the mend, as they fawned over Theodora who seemed delighted to meet another set of grandparents.

Yeah, I thought to myself as I looked around, everything was clearly working out for the best.

And as a pair of arms slid around my waist and pulled me against a hard chest, I couldn't help but smile.

"There's an open bar. What do you say we get drunk and marry each other again?"

"Been there, done that. We should seriously find a new hobby. Plus, I can't drink."

"What?" said Jude. "Is the booze that bad?"

I placed his hand directly over my stomach and asked him, "Did you just think I was getting fat?"

"More like pleasantly plump," he replied, and I turned around and smacked him playfully on his shoulder.

He reached for my hand and placed a kiss on the inside of my palm before bringing both hands up on either side of my thickening waist.

"I'm going to be a dad…" He said softly, all joking aside as he stared at my belly in awe.

"Yeah," was all I could add. I had only found out a week ago, and I was still trying to digest the news.

"If it's a girl, can we name her Ophelia?" It was my turn to swallow hard as I looked up at the man I loved and nodded.

"Or if it's a boy, you can name him Oliver," said my employer, popping up from nowhere.

Oliver had taken a trip to Europe and had strangely made a full recovery from whatever had previously ailed him. He bragged that he had had the best medicine Euros could buy, but I didn't think even Europe could bring a man back from the brink of death. I pretended to believe him.

"I doubt we'll name him Oliver, but good try, Dad," Jude responded.

"An old man can wish," Oliver said, winking at me.

He walked away grinning and I couldn't help but wonder if somehow me, Jude, Vegas, all of this had been his grand plan.

If so, I wasn't angry. I just owed him a thank you.

All thoughts of Oliver's interference—or lack of interference—went out the window as Jude pulled me close and said with a sigh, "I couldn't dream of a better life, Lacey. Thanks for putting up with me."

"You're welcome, and you know it'll only cost you a billion dollars."

"Can I pay it to you over a lifetime?" He took my hand and smiled down at me.

I smiled up at him. "I wouldn't have it any other way."

ALSO BY SUMMER COOPER

DARK DESIRES
~ A billionaire dark romance series ~
Dark Desire
Dark Rules
Dark Secret
Dark Time
Dark Truth

BARRE TO BAR
~ A billionaire second chance series ~
Dancing With Lies
Dancing With Temptation
Dancing With Doubt
Dancing With Guilt
Dancing With Redemption

TWISTED INTENTION
~ A billionaire revenge romance series ~
Twisted Beauty
Twisted Love
Twisted Fate

Mafia's Obsession
~ A hot mafia romance series ~
Mafia's Dirty Secret
Mafia's Fake Bride
Mafia's Final Play

Screaming Demons
~ An MC romance series full of suspense ~
Rough Start
Rough Ride
Rough Choice
Rough Patch
Rough Return
Rough Road
Rough Trip
Rough Night
Rough Love

Standalone Contemporary Romance
Billionaire in Vegas
Billionaire Hunt

Billionaire's Game
Billionaire Retreat
Billionaire On Air
A Chance To Love
Somebody To Love
Not Mine To Love

Check out Summer's entire collection at
www.summercooper.com/books

ABOUT SUMMER COOPER

Thank you so much for reading. Without you, it wouldn't be possible for me to be a full-time author. I hope you enjoy reading my books as much as I do writing them.

Besides (obviously!) reading and writing, I also love cuddling my dogs, shouting at Alexa, being upside down (aka Yoga) and driving my family cray-cray!

Get in touch at
hello@summercooper.com
www.summercooper.com

facebook.com/summercooperauthor
instagram.com/summercooperauthor
goodreads.com/summercooper
bookbub.com/profile/summer-cooper